A

CANDLELIGHT REGENCY SPECIAL

CANDLELIGHT REGENCIES

THE
BRASH AMERICAN

Samantha Lester

A CANDLELIGHT REGENCY SPECIAL

Published by
Dell Publishing Co., Inc.
1 Dag Hammarskjold Plaza
New York, New York 10017

ISBN: 0-440-10945-0

Printed in the United States of America
First printing—February 1981

To Mickey Fitting,
a friend beyond compare

THE
BRASH AMERICAN

CHAPTER ONE

Lady Brinsley touched her daughter's arm to draw the girl's attention. "Can you not stoop slightly, Melissa?" she asked in exasperation.

The girl looked down from her superior height, a smile of irritation on her lips. "No, Mama, I cannot. I should look as if ready to spring upon the males you would have me impressing. I fear you and Father must, in time, admit that I am six feet in height and therefore unacceptable to those you would have as suitors to me."

"Lower your voice," Lady Brinsley whispered, aware of several heads turning to catch the conversation.

Melissa tossed her head in anger, causing her blond hair to whip wildly around her shoulders. A glint of impishness shone in her green eyes as she said, "Your concern over my twenty years and my unattached situation is common knowledge throughout London, Mama. It speaks well for your determination to see the last of your four daughters wed and with children." She paused and sent a glance around the crowd. "I find it difficult to concern myself with the opinions of any who would watch such a demonstration as this with bated breath."

Her mother's frown deepened. "The walk-along, though of German invention, is sure to become popular when your father markets it. Your disdain for it ignores the effect it might have on your dowry."

Melissa chuckled bitterly. "It is nothing but a wood fence rail set on wheels. It will not make walking unnecessary. I should make a fair sight aboard such a thing, I imagine."

The thought of the girl hiking her afternoon gown to straddle the machine being demonstrated brought the color of embarrassment to Lady Brinsley's cheeks. She sent a hasty glance around the crowd to determine who had overheard the brash statement.

"You needn't worry, Mother," Melissa assured her. "Since I am able to scan the entire gathering, I can assure you that no one is aware of my outrageous remarks." She glanced around the crowd, her extreme height allowing her a nearly clear view over the heads of all present. Her eyes came to rest on a man directly across the demonstration glen. She studied him for a long moment, smiling as she noticed that he, alone of the men present, wore loose-legged trousers unpleated at the hips. Her smile increased as he removed his coat, folded it over an arm, and then undid the buttons of his waistcoat. Stern glances of disapproval were sent to him by all who stood near as he ran a hand through his wealth of jet-black hair and changed his stance to a comfortable hip-shot position. "Personal comfort first and the devil with all present," she muttered, admiring the man's uncaring attitude.

"What did you say, Melissa?" her mother demanded.

Sending her glance down to meet her mother's eyes, she shook her head. "Nothing, Mother. It was only a comment on a gentleman across the way." She again looked toward the independent one and found his studious glance on her. Blushing, she averted her eyes and gave her attention to the demonstration. From that moment until the demonstration came to an end, she felt his eyes on her. Then, without looking in his direction, she turned away to accompany her mother to a table in the glen, where refreshments were being served.

Shortly after they had been served tea, her father joined them, saying, "Ah, the walk-along is the talk of all present. The profits on such a thing will be enormous."

"The demonstration went well, I take it, Reginald?" his wife asked. Then, her eyes narrowing, she muttered, "Such an uncouth fellow. Who in the world can he be?"

Following her glance, Melissa saw the uncoated gentleman of her earlier perusal stepping across the glen in their direction. For a moment she thought he meant to approach them, then realized no stranger would be so rash.

"Deuced if I know the fellow," her father said in answer to his wife's query. "No refinement about him for a certainty. With his clothes undone like that he appears to be preparing for bed."

"Or he prefers to be comfortable rather than suffer because of the idiotic rules of society," Melissa said.

Sir Reginald fixed her with a glance. "Your lack of respect for society and its cares do you ill, Missy. It would serve you well if—" He broke off at his wife's gasp and again followed her glance. "By Jove, can the beggar intend to confront us with himself?"

Melissa's head swung in the indicated direction, and she found herself looking up into a pair of laughing gray eyes. For an instant she found herself set aback by the smiling features. Then, with a bow to her, the newcomer said, "Good afternoon, miss. I am Brett Boyden of the United States of America. I noticed you across the glen moments ago and was instantly struck by your beauty. Might I join you?"

Shock registered itself on both her parents' faces. For a moment she hesitated before saying, "It would be unseemly, sir. For we have not been formally introduced. I thank you for your generous compliment, though."

14

He chuckled aloud at the statement. "Ah, England and her straitlaced manners. We are half introduced since I have given you my name. Would it be possible for me to half join you?"

The question brought unbidden laughter to her lips. She blushed for a moment and turned her glance to her father.

"I say, my good man," Sir Reginald began, getting to his feet, "your manners are far from acceptable to me or any of quality in England. You dashed Colonials believe it possible to intrude in any situation and—"

Boyden's shoulders stiffened. He met Brinsley's angry glance, asking, "And do I know you, sir?"

Blood rushed into the older man's face at the interruption. He breathed deeply for a moment, then snapped, "I assure you, sir, you shall if you intend to remain in England, else my name is not Reginald Brinsley."

"Brinsley?" the man repeated. "The name is unknown to me. Is it possible you are the sire of this lovely maiden?"

"You, sir, are uncouth to the ultimate," Brinsley growled. "Take yourself from our presence before I am forced to have you removed."

Chuckling, Boyden sent a glance around the glen. After a moment of such perusal, he again met Brinsley's angry glance. "I doubt any present would care." He paused, his glance shifting to Melissa and the near smile on her lips. Suddenly,

15

turning back to Sir Reginald, he bowed slightly and said, "My apologies, sir. Being unused to the ways of your country, I seem to have over-stepped."

With a bow to Lady Brinsley he turned for a second to Melissa, smiled at her as if to say "Another time," and left them.

"Such an odious person," Lady Brinsley said, watching the intruder's receding back.

"Indeed," her husband agreed. "Colonists are all alike. No respect for anyone."

"But," Melissa said, her eyes following the recent visitor, "he knows his own mind and needs no one to make apology for him."

"Well, the dolt is gone," her father said. "Let us drink our tea. Ashley Currante is even now taking orders for the walk-along."

CHAPTER TWO

As the afternoon waned into evening, Melissa grew tried of the bustle of persons around her. Looking at her mother, she asked, "Might we return home, Mother? I feel neither of us is doing our health well."

Sighing, Lady Brinsley nodded. "I, too, feel the weight of the day in my system, Melissa. Come, let us walk to the carriage. Your father will follow when the business is seen to."

"He was decidedly different from any of my acquaintances," Melissa said as she followed her mother toward the carriage.

"Of whom are you speaking?" the older woman asked, stepping into the vehicle and seating herself.

"Mr. Boyden of the United States, Mother. Did you not think him a refreshing change from the dandies who populate the streets of London?"

"Hummph! The likes of him are an unwelcome quantity in England. Take your thoughts from him. If you must think along such lines, put your efforts toward an acceptable mate. As your father often comments you are nearing the point of spinsterhood."

Melissa laughed bitterly. "And who would you have me wed, Mother? Is it not the custom to await a marriage offer before becoming betrothed?" The bitter laugh came again. "Those few gentlemen Father has pressed into being my escort to the theater spend their time attempting to become invisible for fear they will look ridiculous next to me."

A scolding expression crossed her mother's face. "If you choose to wait for someone taller than yourself, you shall never marry." She shook her head in despair. "Of all born, why is it you should draw the likeness and stature of your great-grandmother?"

Melissa stiffened under the words. "Grandmother is of her own mind in spite of her eighty-odd years. Would that I could be like her in every way. As to my being over-particular in my choice of men, I am not. I care not for a man's height if he does not. As grandmother did, I shall marry a man I can love, no matter what his height—if he is beyond caring about mine."

Exasperation had its way with Lady Brinsley. "There is no one who would not be conscious of the difference, child. Set your mind upon it. You must of necessity hope that one of your association takes a fancy to you. Otherwise you shall, indeed, see your life spent as a spinster. Now clear your mind of such matters. We near home. Your father will wish our opinions of what we have heard concerning the walk-along this day."

"Tish on the dratted machine," Melissa answered, piqued at her mother's attitude. "Anyone who would be seen on such a contraption must be near to taking leave of his senses." She turned her face away, forestalling any further conversation with her mother.

Moments later the carriage turned into the circular drive and came to a stop at the front stoop of Brinsley House. Lady Brinsley, irritation obvious in her manner, stepped from the coach and made her way into the house. Melissa, a smile of understanding riding her features, followed.

Rosalin, the governess who ofttimes Melissa felt was closer than her own mother, greeted them as they entered. "And milady Brinsley, did the demonstration go well?"

Lady Brinsley nodded and favored the hired woman with a smile. "Quite well, Rosalin. Though I sense you have been amiss in your teachings of Melissa. She does exasperate one on occasion."

The governess's glance shifted to the smiling girl. "Ah, Missy," she chided, "what devilment have you been up to this day?"

Melissa shrugged and stepped past the two older women, saying, "The discussion of the day has again turned to my height and my unmarried status, Rosy. It appears that I shall go to my grave unwed if Mother is correct in her reasoning." She left them then to make her way up the stairs to her room.

Behind her her mother faced the governess with her color high. "You must speak with your charge, Rosalin. She tests the patience of her father and me at every turn. She seems little concerned for her station or her future. She must be made to realize what is expected of ladies such as herself."

Rosalin nodded in understanding. "I shall assist her with her bath, milady. If it is in me to do so, I shall convince her of her duties to herself and her family." With a slight bow she left Lady Brinsley to follow in Melissa's wake.

Melissa turned from removing her shirtwaist as Rosalin opened the door and stepped in. The girl frowned at the grimace on the woman's face and asked, "And what is it my mother has ordered you to do that causes you to look so, Rosalin?"

"Ah, that woman," the governess said. "She has instructed me to bring you to heel on the matters of your duty as a lady." The grimacing expression left her face then, and she added, "I doubt there is a need for such doings, though. You are unlike your sisters in every way, child. I sometimes worry about you and your future."

"As Mama worries?" Melissa asked.

The governess shook her head. "Not as she worries, but as one who has seen to your needs since the day you were born. I, like your parents, would have you married and happy."

"And I shall be when a man appears who cares nothing of my height and only for me." Her features hardened then. "I will not wed anyone I do not love, Rosy. I will not."

"And I would not ask you to, child. Lord knows there are plenty who see only money and position as reasons for wedlock. I would not have you share the unhappiness they know. You must, however, realize that you are of an age where marriage is expected. Aye, and by most it is a desired thing. Truly you must also realize the—"

"—the lack of suitors who would wish to be seen with one who is of a height above their own?" the girl snapped. "I do realize both these things, Rosy. But I would rather spend my remaining days as a spinster than marry simply to answer the demands of society."

The governess smiled slightly. "And this, I assume, is what has your mother in such a tizzy at the moment." She shook her head in mock scolding. "Ah, child, when will you learn to restrain your tongue concerning your ideas?"

"You are wrong," Melissa informed her. "Mother is incensed simply because I found a gentleman attractive in certain respects. She considers him a crashing boor."

"A gentleman?" the governess asked, a quizzical

expression on her features. "I cannot believe your mother would take offense at any gentleman you found to your liking. Her desire to see you wed would overpower any notion of dislike."

The girl laughed happily at the statement. "It was a Colonist, Rosy," she said in a conspiratorial manner. "He is brash beyond compare. And his sense of what is humorous is fantastic. I should like to meet him."

"And his bearing, child. What of it?"

"You mean, is he as tall as I? No. Shorter by a good two inches, unless I misguess. But though surely he was aware of my height, he did approach our table at the glen and introduce himself. He further asked permission to join us."

"He what?" the governess exclaimed.

Melissa nodded. "He did, Rosy. Oh, he is not of the ilk the dandies of my acquaintance are. He strikes one as being a shade beyond the independent." She paused for a moment as if in deep thought. "It comes to me that he is attractive in a way I've never known a man to be before now. I do believe I should like to make Mr. Boyden's further acquaintance."

"Boyden?" Rosy asked. "A common name unless I misguess. And he attempted to force himself into your presence without the benefit of an introduction?"

"Only halfway," the girl answered with a laugh, then proceeded to relate the incident to the governess. "He is unique," she added upon finishing the tale. "Yes, I should like to know the man better."

"Hummph! I doubt that the chance shall be yours. It would seem from what you say that your father saw to the putting down of the beggar. And, if I may say so, Missy, it is for the better. The Colonies are populated by all sorts of thieves and brigands. They live a life totally different from what we know."

"And are happy in it, I would wager. Oh, that I might have the opportunity to visit the new-formed country. They say one may look for miles at a time without seeing another soul. It must quicken the heartbeat of all who live there."

"If wild beasts and equally wild men quicken the heartbeat, I sense you are correct. I would not care to face such things myself. Now enough of this. We must see to your bath. Your father will return from the demonstration soon."

Melissa allowed her to assist in the removal of her clothing. Then, as she sank into the tub, she said, "The walk-along was a tremendous success, according to Father, Rosy. It seems but an idiotic toy to me."

"That being the case, you must dress for company at dinner, child. For, unless I misguess, the young gentleman who represents your father will be present."

"You refer to Ashley, Rosy?" Melissa asked, and

at the other's nod she said, "Then you are mistaken. He is neither a gentleman nor young. He is in search of only that which will bring him wealth and position in society. For those two things I feel he would sever his mother's head from her body."

The governess's eyes widened at the ferocity of the statement. "Child, child," she exclaimed, "how you do go on. Mr. Currante has an eye out for his future, it is to be admitted, but you exaggerate. He is a gentleman and while not of the titled class, he appears to be a man of some means."

"He is thirty-five years of age," Melissa said, "and he has spent every waking moment of that time figuring methods to use on others to increase his wealth."

"As do most of those who attend to business" was the retort. "Now enough of this. Scrub yourself and don the yellow muslin. It will please everyone at dinner, no matter what their desires or ends." She turned toward the wardrobe as the girl began soaping herself. Moments later she said, as if talking to herself, "Mr. Currante is of a height surpassing your own, child."

"Oh, by all that's holy!" Melissa groaned. "Is height all anyone in this house can think of? Should I marry an ogre simply because he is of a height greater than mine? Well, I will not. Besides, thank goodness, he has made no such advances toward me. It would gain him nothing at this time. Pray it never will." She returned to her soaping, her mood darkening as thoughts of the man under discussion filled her head. Finally she rinsed the soap from her body and stepped from the tub.

"As always, you are all legs, child," Rosy said, handing her a towel. "Though all parts of your body are in proportion and attractive, it is beyond me why the good Lord chose to lengthen your legs to such a degree."

Accepting the towel, Melissa moved to stand before a mirror and study herself as she removed the moisture from her skin. "In spite of my height and the length of leg you mention, Rosy, I feel I am above average. My bosom, while not of such dimensions to tip me forward, is not small by any notion." She turned to face the mirror and added, "And there is nothing about the rest of my body that I believe to be without attractiveness."

"You are a lovely young lady," Rosy answered. "But it ill behooves you to preen in front of the mirror without garments covering your nakedness. Don your clothing and allow me to assist you, else you shall be late arriving for dinner. You know how that irritates your father."

"I know, Rosy," Melissa answered. Turning from the mirror, she met the older woman's glance for a moment and took heed of an alien expression in that face. Her own problems left her mind for the moment, and she asked, "What is it, Rosy? The expression you wear surely cannot be concern for my never ending situation. Something else is bothering you."

Rosy hesitated, then nodded. "Aye, child. You are correct. It is my youngest sister in Essex. She has taken to her bed, ill beyond belief. There is no one but her man to watch over the children and care for the house."

Instant sympathy swept over Melissa. "Ah, Rosy, and I, in my own self pity, was oblivious of your problems. You shall go to your sister at once. There is nothing here that cannot be done by someone else. Besides, since I am in my twentieth year, I sense it is past time that I learn to see to my own needs."

"Oh, child," Rosy protested, "I could not. Why, you—"

"—will survive, Rosy. The question is settled. When dressed, I shall call a carriage for you and inform Mother that you are to be gone until the matter of your sister and her family is improved. Go this instant and prepare a bag. I will see to my own dinner preparations."

Reluctantly the governess said, "Though it is not my desire to leave you, child, it would serve my mind well to know the depth of my sister's problems and assist her if I can. I thank you for your concern. I will be gone no longer than necessary," She turned to leave the room.

26

"You will remain with your sister until all is again well with her, Rosy," Melissa ordered. "And see to it that you spend no time worrying of me. I will be fine."

CHAPTER THREE

The yellow muslin rustled lightly around her an̄-
kles as Melissa made her way down the stairs to
the rear of the house. Entering the kitchen, she
caught the attention of a servant and gave instruc-
tions for a carriage to be prepared to carry the
governess on her journey. That done, she left in
search of her mother so that she might inform her
of the emergency. As she passed the library the
sound of men's voices caught her attention.
"Drat," she muttered, recognizing the oily tones
of her father's representative, Ashley Currante.
Her mood was depressed when she entered the
dining room and gave her mother the information.

"Why, of course she shall go, Melissa," Lady
Brinsley agreed. "There has been none as faithful
as Rosalin." Stepping back a pace, she studied her
daughter with an evaluating eye. "I must say,
Melissa, you look very nice. Could it be you wish
to attract the attention of someone who will be
dining at our table tonight?"

Sighing heavily, the girl shook her head in a
negative answer. "Mother, I have no desire to attract the attention of either you or father. And if
you refer to Ashley Currante, it would suit me

well if my eyes never fell upon him again. I would like to dine in my room, if I may."

The pleased expression left her mother's face. "You certainly may not," she snapped. "You will attend the meal with the rest of us. You will not insult Mr. Currante by refusing to dine in his presence. He, though not of the titled, would be a worthy catch for any girl. You would do well to consider that in light of your present situation."

The angry retort that rose to the girl's lips died as her father and the man in question entered the dining room. Turning at the sound of their voices, she forced a smile to her lips and asked, "Father, Mr. Currante, did the day go well?"

"Beyond our dreams," her father answered, a satisfied smile on his face. "Ashley has already made the walk-along an institution in London."

Her eyes met the black piercing ones of the man in question. For an instant she felt repulsion clutch at her stomach. Then he was bowing from the waist to her.

"Melissa," he said, "yellow becomes you. You are lovely."

Resisting the urge to turn away from him, she said, "Thank you, Mr. Currante. You are too kind."

He sighed and shook his head. "Melissa, when will you elect to call me by my given name? I am, after all, anything but a stranger to your family."

"I intend no disrespect," she answered and

knew from the glint in his eye that he was aware of her lie. "I was taught to respect my elders. It is a habit that clings to one."

The reference to the difference in their ages forced the man's eyes to narrow. A tight smile took his lips as he nodded. "You impressed at least one individual at the demonstration today, Melissa. A commoner from America approached me, seeking information of you."

A picture of Brett Boyden leaped into her mind at the words. Blood flowed to her face and she found herself at a loss for words. She was grateful her father chose that moment to suggest they take their places at the dining table.

"Now, Ashley," Sir Reginald said when they had all seated themselves, "what was it you were saying about someone taking note of Melissa?"

Currante cleared his throat and leveled a glance at Melissa. "It seems a rather uncouth fellow named Boyden took a fancy to our Melissa. He approached me asking questions of the family and of your place of residence. Upon realizing that he was of the lower class, I ignored him. There were others, however, who might have given him the information he sought."

"Boyden? Boyden?" Brinsley muttered. "Oh, yes, the blighter from the glen this afternoon. Very forward sort, as I recall. No manners whatsoever. Approached us and requested permission to join us. No sense of the common decencies. Typical of the Colonists."

"He had the effrontery to force himself upon you?" Currante asked.

"Not effrontery, sir," Melissa snapped, anger filling her expression. "He was kind enough to pay me a fine compliment. The fact that he has little knowledge of our severe ways does not change the fact that he is, in my opinion, a gentleman."

The representative laughed shortly. "Perhaps in America he is known as a gentleman, Melissa. I fear, however, he is an oaf of the first water." The black eyes narrowed slightly, and he added, "And he certainly would have had to crane his neck to look into your eyes."

Harsh color flooded her face. She pushed back her chair, saying, "I am sick to the death of references to my height. And, sir, Mr. Boyden approached me while I was seated. If he had chosen such time when I was standing, I feel certain it would have made no difference to him. He is, in spite of implications to the contrary, anything but an oaf." She turned from the table, saying, "I feel my appetite has fled. I would—"

She was interrupted by a servant, who stepped into the room saying, "Sir Reginald, the—"

"You need not announce me, Robert," a commanding voice said. The next moment an extremely tall woman with steel-gray hair, regal bearing, and sharp green eyes, much like Melissa's, pushed the servant aside and entered the room. Her eyes took in all present. "I doubt there's anyone of importance here who need be reminded of my name."

Melissa was the first to react to the intrusion. A smile taking her features, she rushed forward to encircle the old woman with her arms. "Grandmother!" she exclaimed, placing her lips on the aged cheek. "Oh, I am so happy to see you."

"Hummph!" the woman snorted. "Then I'll wager you are the only one in this household who is. How are you, Missy?"

"Grandmama!" Sir Reginald got out, getting to his feet. "We had no notice you were coming. I—"

"You are an idiot," the woman snapped. "Much like your father, as I recall. He never could conceal his irritation at my presence." She turned to a stunned Lady Brinsley, saying, "Edith, you are beginning to show your age. Your open mouth does little to alleviate the picture. I have not eaten, nor has my driver."

Stuttering in near panic, Lady Brinsley got to her feet muttering, "Of course, Grandmother. I—"

"—will allow a good man to starve unless he is taken to the kitchen and fed," the regal one interrupted. "Lord, when I think I'm responsible for— Well, never mind. My luggage is in the carriage. Have someone see to it."

32

"At once, Grandmother," Sir Reginald said, hurrying from the room.

Currante sat staring at the old woman, his expression one of complete disbelief. She swung her attention to him, demanding, "And is there something you wish to say to me, sir?"

"I—I—" he stuttered.

"Uh . . . Grandmother," Lady Brinsley said as if in fear of her life, "this is Ashley Currante, Reginald's chief representative. Ashley, this is my husband's grandmother, the Duchess of Rutherford."

Instant respect replaced all other expressions on the man's face. He stood, bowing from the waist. "Your Grace," he got out, "I have heard of you since I was a child. I—"

"—appear to be of the solicitor's breed," she cut in. "I find that distasteful." She turned her attention to Melissa, who stood beside her. The old eyes softened as she studied the girl for a long moment. Then, in a voice barely loud enough for the girl to hear, she asked, "You were in high anger when I entered, child. What is it?"

Sending a glance in her mother's direction, Melissa shrugged and answered. "It is nothing for you to concern yourself with, Grandmother. Only a continuing problem that seems never to end."

"We shall discuss it at length when I've eaten," the duchess told her in no uncertain terms. Then, turning back to Lady Brinsley, she said, "Edith, your servants are amiss. I see but four settings on the table."

Flushing, Lady Brinsley left her place at the table, calling for servants as she moved. Moments later, when a fifth place had been set, she turned to the duchess, saying, "Had we but known you were coming, Grandmother, we would have—"

"Pah!" the duchess exclaimed. "I am not your grandmother and I choose not to be referred to as such by you. What are we eating tonight?"

Sir Reginald reentered the room at that moment to report that her baggage had been moved to an upstairs room and that her driver was being fed. "He shall have his fill in our kitchen, Grandmama," he assured her.

"Which is more than I can be certain of," she retorted. Then, moving to the place set for her, she seated herself and fixed Currante with a searching stare.

For several moments he withstood the glare of those green eyes, then he dropped his glance. Color rising in his face, he asked, "Is there something I have done, your Grace?"

"Hummph!" she snorted. "And how would I know that? Since I have only this moment made your acquaintance, I have no way of knowing anything you have or have not done." She turned her attention from him to Melissa, who still stood at the end of the table. "What is it, child?" she demanded. "Have you completed the meal?"

Smiling in spite of her efforts to the contrary, the girl answered, "No, Grandmother. I had decided to forgo the meal this evening."

"Nonsense. You will sit here beside me. It has been several years since I laid eyes on you. Come, seat yourself."

Melissa, a smile still on her face, moved to take her place at the table. "I am glad you are here," she said, gaining the seat. "There is much I would discuss with you."

"All in good time, child, all in good time. Now I would have some food. It seems my driver fares better than I do. I am sure there is a precedent for such a thing, but I do not care to know of it."

When the food was placed before them, Lady Brinsley again took her seat, her face flushed, her manner nervous. "And," she asked at length, "what is it that brings you from the country, Duchess?"

"The same carriage that has taken me all places for the past sixty-five years," the duchess answered.

"I meant—"

"Edith meant the reason for your visit, Grandmother," Sir Reginald finished for his wife. "We had no notion you planned a visit. Why, it has been—let me see—how long has it been?"

"It was on the occasion of Marion's marriage to that asinine Lord Fairbanks," the old woman said.

"That was, for the most part, a wasted journey. How are the girls?"

Brinsley straightened his shoulders and allowed an expression of pride to cross his features. "They are doing quite well, Grandmother. And Lord Fairbanks, in spite of what you believe, is doing quite well in his business of breeding fine horses."

"Hummph! He could do as well by merely saving the constant and never ending dowry you bargained him into marriage with. Ah, well, there are few of the old duke's blood who have the intelligence he had."

Reginald Brinsley reddened. His glance shifted to Ashley Currante momentarily, then he said, "Grandmother, your opinion of any dowry is well-known. Did Edith tell you that Ashley is my chief representative?"

"She did" was the answer. "She did not, however, inform me of his duties." The green eyes settled on Currante's face. "Tell me, sir, what exactly is it you do for my grandson?"

Currante looked first at his employer, then met the older woman's searching glance. "I market and sell the merchandise Sir Reginald chooses to handle, your Grace. I attempt only to do my utmost toward improving the business and seeing to Sir Brinsley's pleasure."

She was silent for a long moment, then her glance swung to her grandson and from there to Melissa. Finally she said, "Well, it seems the food grows cool. I detest cool food." With that she began to eat.

Sir Reginald sighed audibly as he, too, began eating. Sending an embarrassed glance at Currante, he shrugged as if to say, There's nothing one can do.

Currante ate quietly, his thoughts obviously elsewhere. Several times his glance moved to capture Melissa's personage, then his eyes were averted. Midway through the meal he was lifting a bite of pork to his mouth when the duchess's voice stopped him.

"And are you married, Mr. Currante?" she asked.

The pork suspended on his fork, he shook his head. "No, your Grace. Business has become a mistress of mine, I fear. It leaves little time for thoughts of personal pleasure."

"But you do have plans of wedding, do you not?"

"Grandmother," Sir Reginald said, "I am afraid Ashley is taken aback by your manner. He knows nothing of your ways. Your personal questions do, I'm certain, seem an intrusion."

"No, Sir Reginald," Currante said. "It is all right. Though I admit the straightforward manner in which the duchess attacks a question is unique, I feel she deserves an answer." He swung his glance to the older woman, an expression of patience on his face. "To be correct, your Grace, I do have

37

plans of marriage, but not in the near future. The lady I have decided on for my mate is as yet unaware of my plans. When I am ready, I shall inform her of the role she is to play."

The old eyes narrowed at the statement. "Of the role she is to play?" she echoed. "You feel this woman will allow you such control over her future?"

The smile remained at his lips, as if frozen there. "Marriage, like anything else a person undertakes, should be a business matter, your Grace. She will acknowledge that fact when the moment arrives for me to state my troth."

The duchess turned to face her grandson, her manner harsh, her eyes alight. "Reginald, you have a conceited ass for a representative. Your judgment of people has, obviously, remained the same since childhood." She turned to the meal again without further word.

With the exception of the sharp inhalation of breath by Lady Brinsley, a dead silence held the table in its grasp. Suddenly, anger and color flooding his features, Currante pushed back his chair, wiped at his lips with his napkin, and said, "Sir Reginald, I sense my presence here is a cause of discomfort to the duchess. I would take my leave of this gathering, if I may."

Brinsley, shock registering on his face, got to his feet hurriedly. His irritation was plain when he said, "Grandmother, you are in my home. For you to insult a guest of mine in such a manner is outrageous. I will not—"

"—speak to me in such a way," the duchess snapped. "If I have injured your representative's senses, I apologize. I do not, however, believe such a thing is possible. He is a man without feeling except for a desire for wealth and power. His anger stems from the fact that he feels I might cost him an opportunity at that wealth and power, nothing else. As to your reference to your home, this house—as the others—remains a portion of the dukedom. Until my death it shall be so. If your Mr. Currante wishes to take offense at the truth, then have the good manners to see him to the door. My food cools." She returned to her eating, ignoring everyone around the table.

Currante waited no longer. Throwing his napkin forcefully to his plate, he turned and stomped from the room. Moments later, before Brinsley could marshal his thoughts enough to follow him, the sound of the front door banging shut came to them.

The duchess brought her attention from her plate and smiled, saying, "Ah, it is always such a pleasure for one of my years to enjoy the company of her family at a meal. Tell me, Reginald, how goes the business?"

Mouth agape, Brinsley stared at her. "Grandmother," he got out finally, "how could . . . I shall speak to Father of this matter. I will not allow you to commit such a thing."

She nodded. "I'm certain the young duke will bend an attentive ear to your complaints, Reginald. Your grandfather guessed that he would be the more doltish of his children. However, you had best realize that while he is duke in name, it is in name only. The old duke saw to that when he determined that we were to have nothing but sons and grandsons of questionable abilities." She turned to Lady Brinsley, the smile again taking her old face. "Edith, your home, as always, is immaculate. And such a lovely dress. Is it new?"

Lady Brinsley started at the question. Her eyes flew to her husband's florid face. Then, over his stuttering, she answered, "Yes, your Grace, I only yesterday received it from the seamstress."

"Excellent," the duchess returned. "The color brings out the best of your features." She turned to Melissa, who sat with a hand covering her mouth. "And what is bothering you, child?"

Coughing back outright laughter, the girl met her great-grandmother's sparkling eyes. "Only a bit of food caught in my throat, Grandmother. It is nothing."

"Well, let us complete the meal. I tire after my journey. I would take to my quarters at the earliest. Missy, I would speak with you following dinner."

"Yes, Grandmother," Melissa said, an imp of devilment playing in her eyes. "I shall be happy to attend you in your room."

The rest of the meal was spent in silence. Sir Reginald, for his portion, found his appetite stemmed to nothing. Lady Brinsley picked at the food on her plate as if in doubt of its quality. Finally the duchess sighed heavily and pushed back from the table, announcing, "As usual, Edith, you retain the finest of cooks. The meal was delightful." She got to her feet and, with a nod to all present, left the room.

No sooner had she left the dining room than Sir Reginald growled deeply in his throat. "I shall speak with Father of this matter," he said. "Though duchess she be and grandmother of mine, I will not allow her to carry on so." He stood, his glance on his wife. "I must at this moment search out Ashley and tender my apologies for the treatment he received at her hands. I shall return when I have seen to it." He was nearing the doorway when he turned and, as if in afterthought, said, "Melissa, it will not be necessary to mention to Grandmother that I am seeking Ashley. She would not understand."

Suppressing a chuckle at her father's obvious discomfiture, the girl nodded. "Yes, Father. I shall keep your secret."

He stood for a long moment staring at her. Then with an oath, he turned, mumbling, "Why

41

couldn't I have been blessed with at least one son?" Then he was gone.

"Melissa," Lady Brinsley scolded, "your actions toward your father are ill conceived. Your love for the duchess is of no secret to anyone, though how you can come to such a thought escapes me. You must, however, remember your place."

"Place?" Melissa demanded. "My place, except with Grandmother, seems to be as a whipping boy for my sin of not taking a husband. I mean no slight, Mother, but it would seem I am like Grandmother in more ways than simply height and appearance." She stood up and prepared to leave the table. "I would attend her now, if I may. Her age is such that she surely retires early."

"Would that her manner of overbearance retire itself permanently," Lady Brinsley said. Then with a nod she added, "Very well. Go to her. And, child, if it is within your power as her favorite, speak to her of the anguish she causes all who incur her sharp tongue."

Unable to control a smile at the plea, Melissa nodded. "Yes, Mama. I shall attempt to persuade her not to chew on those she loves." She left the room then, her shoulders shaking in silent laughter as she made her way up the winding staircase. She was chuckling audibly by the time she reached the door of the master guest room and knocked.

"Enter" came the order from within.

Stepping into the room, Melissa swung her

glance around until it settled on the duchess, who lay in the huge bed with the satin covers up to her chin. Moving forward, the young woman bent to place a kiss on the old lady's cheek. "Grandmother, you would anger the saints with your actions. You have Father and Mother in a dither unmatched in my experience. Why do you carry on so?"

The smile on the duchess's face belied the snort she gave at the words. "Why, child," she said, "you are as aware as I that everyone in this family considers me senile beyond words. I would have it no other way. Under such a charge, I impart the truth to those who are too blind in their own love of self to see it. Now, what is about in this house that had you in such straits when I entered?"

"It is nothing, Grandmother. I would hear of your time since you were last here."

The old woman fixed the girl with a steady glance. "I tire, Missy. If you persist in denying me the opportunity to assist you with your problem, then I shall of necessity sleep." She turned her head away. "Extinguish the lamp as you go, child."

"Now stop that, Grandmother," Melissa orderd, a smile on her face. "Perhaps the others do not realize it, but I know you to be a fraud. Very well, I will bare my woes to you. But there is nothing you or anyone can do, for Father and

Mother will be themselves in the matter until I am wed."

"Wed? You plan on being wed and have not mentioned it to me?" An expression of hurt took the old features.

Melissa laughed aloud. "No, no, Grandmother. I have not the least hope of wedding anyone. It is that fact that so upsets Mother and Father. They let no day pass without reminding me that I am of a height to be undesirable to any man. They would, if I were to allow it, purchase a husband for me as they did for my sisters."

The duchess sat upright in the bed. "Undesirable height? What utter nonsense is this I hear? Your parents are truly asinine. Why, you are of a height less than my own. Do they believe my father bought the duke's hand in marriage to me?"

The outburst sent Melissa into peals of laughter. When she had controlled herself, she shook her head. "No, Grandmother. They only feel that you are unique. They feel there is no one in the present day who would marry one taller than himself as the duke did you." Her expression sobered suddenly and she added, "They do press me overhard to make a choice for my marriage. When I dare to mention my desire to love the man I marry and have him return that love, I am informed that no one of less stature than I could care in such a way."

"Stupid, unthinking asses," the old woman

snapped. "And, tell me, child. Is there someone you feel love in your heart for?"

Again the girl shook her head. "No, Grandmother. There is no one. And unless such a being comes upon the scene, I would rather spend my days as a spinister. It is beyond thinking that I spend the rest of my life with someone I do not care for."

"Well spoken, child. Well, we shall see to your parents' idiotic reasoning. The old duke and I were happy beyond expression for all our years together. There is none could question our love for each other, though he was of a height four inches less than my own. Utter nonsense rules this house I swear!"

Though agreeing with the old woman, Melissa hastened to quiet her. "Grandmother, remember your years. You must not become upset over such trivial matters. You will—"

"—outlive all who consider me in my dotage," the duchess told her. "Had I been as you suggest, the two-day trip in my carriage would have seen to me. Bah! Age is a quantity I have no time for. What matters is the situation into which you are being forced."

A puzzled expression captured the girl's face. "I am being forced into no situation, Grandmother. I have said it is only their constant remarks as to my unwed state and my height that become irritating."

The old head shook in despair. "Ah, child, you lack the experience necessary to see what is happening. Even stone can be worn away to nothing when water constantly assails it. Your days of independence near an end, unless I misguess."

Melissa's lips set in a stubborn line. "They shall not force me into a marriage such as my sisters know. I will not be a party to such a thing."

"And are your sisters unhappy with their lots?"

"Not unhappy, Grandmother. They have, I feel, done as many do. They have accepted their lots and have decided to forgo satisfaction of the heart. I will not accept that for myself."

"You certainly shall not," the duchess agreed with vengeance. "What of this Currante person? Does he suggest a hint of romance to your mind?"

The question brought laughter to the girl's lips again. Shaking her head, she said, "Oh, no, Grandmother. I find him almost unbearable. Though your way of speaking your thoughts concerning him was unmannerly, to say the least, my opinion matches yours."

The old eyes narrowed slightly. "But not the opinion of your parents," she said as if reading the girl's thoughts. "They have suggested him as a mate to you, have they not?"

"How could you know that, Grandmother?" Melissa asked, amazed at the older woman's insight.

"Tish and tuffle. It is the obvious thing for

them to do. The man is greedy. Your father, whether he would admit it or not, recognizes the trait and admires it. Besides, the man is of a height besting your own. That alone would be sufficient reason for their suggestion that you take him as a husband."

The girl nodded, her eyes downcast. "It has been suggested, Grandmother. Only this evening, Mother pointed out, truthfully enough, that Ashley would be a fair catch for any woman. He will be wealthy, as you suggested. And I cannot argue with the thought that many women would find him attractive."

"But you, being of normal common sense, do not find him so."

"I loathe the man, Grandmother. He features himself something of . . . Oh, I don't know how to explain it. His words concerning the woman he plans to wed do more to describe him than I could. I find him and his words of derision at anyone interested in me despicable."

"There is one who, in spite of your mother's convictions, finds interest in you?" the duchess asked, a questioning glint taking her eyes. "Tell me of him."

Relieved to speak of anything other than Currante, Melissa took a seat on the edge of the bed, saying, "It is nothing really, Grandmother. It occurred today at the demonstration of a fool piece of machinery that Father sponsored. A gentleman from the Colonies, a commoner I understand, took notice of me. In spite of my superior height he approached our table in the glen and introduced himself." She chuckled, remembering the incident, and added, "He had the effrontery to ask if he might join us."

The duchess laughed with her for a moment before saying, "By all that's holy, I find myself puzzled that Edith was not taken with the vapors. Did you find this barbarous fellow attractive, Missy?"

Color rose to the girl's cheeks. "Grandmother, you do pry into one's thoughts. I cannot say whether I found him attractive or not. I only know that he showed little respect for the rigid rules of our society. That alone endeared him to me. I suppose I deserve chastising for such an attitude."

The duchess sat quietly for a long moment, studying the girl. Then, her features settling into lines of relaxation, she asked, "And did this brigand have a name, Melissa?"

Melissa was pulled from her thoughts of the day by the question. "What? Oh, yes, of course, Grandmother. Mr. Brett Boyden." She laughed again, then added, "When I made mention of the fact that he could not join us because we had not been properly introduced, he asked if he could half join us since, having given his name, we were half introduced. I found his humor infectious."

"Boyden?" the duchess repeated the name. "Boyden? That was the name you used. You say he is a commoner?"

Melissa nodded. "Being from the Colonies, he must—in father's thoughts—be nothing more. I have no idea what his station is in America."

"Boyden," the old woman repeated, settling back to the pillow in a thoughtful manner. "The name touches a memory that I cannot at this moment draw to the light. Well, I tire now, child. We shall speak of this again on the morrow. Go now and allow me to rest."

"Yes, Grandmother," Melissa said, bending to again place a kiss on the cheek of her favorite person in all the world. "And thank you for coming." She hesitated a moment. "What reason was there for your taking a trip of such extended time, Grandmother? Did someone summon you?"

The duchess waved a hand negligently. "It is beyond explanation even to myself, child. It occurred to me but two days ago that I should make the trip here. Whatever intelligence it was that so directed me, I am grateful. That, too, is something I shall explain to you on the morrow. Now take yourself from this room so that I might partake of necessary rest." She turned her head away as Melissa blew out the lamp and left the room. "Good night, child. Sleep well," she said softly as the girl pulled the door shut.

CHAPTER FOUR

Upon leaving the house that same evening, Sir Reginald called for his carriage and made his way to his offices in the business district of the city. There he spent several minutes searching through a journal of employee information. Then, with the address of his representative lodged firmly in his mind, he again took to the road and, thirty minutes later, found himself in front of a building in the lower-class section of the city. Repeating the address mentally, he left the carriage and made his way up a set of aged steps to the door bearing the number he had gleaned from the records. Hesitantly he raised a fist and knocked.

"Who's there?" came the demand from within.

"Ashley," Brinsley called, holding his voice down as much as possible, "it is Reginald Brinsley. I would have words with you concerning what has passed this eve."

A moment's silence followed his words, then the door was thrown open and Currante stood facing him. "Sir Reginald," the man said with a sweep of his hand, indicating that Brinsley should enter. "I had no notion of your visit. Whatever is your reason for coming here?"

Brinsley stepped past him. "I am here to tender apology to you for the actions of my grandmother, Ashley. It is with my deepest and most sincere apology that I say I am sorry. She is not pleasant when taken by one of her moods."

An expression of triumph crossed the representative's face as he closed the door and turned to seat his visitor. The expression vanished when Brinsley faced him. Currante hurried to his side. "And could I take your coat, sir?" he asked.

With a glance of more than slight surprise around the humble room, Brinsley shook his head. "I do not intend to stay, Ashley. I only felt that you should receive the apologies of my family for the treatment you have received this evening. The duchess is, without fail, rude beyond the measure. There is none who can call halt to her once she sets her mind to such actions."

"Your apologies are unnecessary, sir," Currante answered, moving forward. "I sympathize with the duchess in her dotage and her loss of manners. Could I get you refreshment, sir?"

"Nothing," Brinsley answered. "And for God's sake, Ashley, do not ever allow Grandmama to hear you express those thoughts in her presence. She is, I fear, convinced that she is yet as young as she was fifty years ago." He paused, his eyes darting around the room. "This apartment—it lacks that which I expected of your residence. Are you in need, man?"

Currante colored slightly, but met his employer's eyes squarely. "Not at all, sir. However, as you are aware, the job I do requires most of my daylight hours. With an eye to my future I took these rooms. One can sleep anyplace as long as one has a proper bed and the necessities when he awakens. I saw no reason to squander my income on the frivolities of a royal apartment."

Brinsley considered the explanation for several moments before nodding appreciatively. "Well done, Ashley. A man should conserve all he can toward the future. The head you have on your shoulders will take you far." Moving to a straightback chair, he lowered himself and fixed the man with a glance. "Will you seek employment elsewhere because of this evening, Ashley?"

An expression of puzzlement swept over the representative's face. "New employment, sir?" he asked. "Whatever for? Are you in some manner displeased with me?"

A tension seemed to drain from Brinsley's face at the question. He shook his head almost violently in negative answer. "Not at all. I only thought— That is, had I been in your place this day, I would have been repulsed at the thought of such insult."

Currante laughed softly. "Ah, sir, do not concern yourself. The duchess, while sharp of tongue, is an amazing woman. I judge her to be in her eighties. . . . " He paused a moment until Brinsley nodded in agreement. "And being such, she is to be excused the normal niceties of normal people. I admit to feeling anger and embarrassment at the moment of her attack on me, but I assure you, the feeling lasted for only a moment. I am sorry you felt obliged to make such an inconvenient trip on my behalf."

"Your understanding of the situation only proves what I have claimed for the past year, Ashley. You are a fine, discerning businessman who will go far. I shouldn't wonder that if you continue in your present vein you will be rewarded with an increase in your salary within another year."

Currante chuckled softly. "Ah, sir, I do not feel worthy of such a statement. I only attempt to do my best as your representative."

"Nonsense," Brinsley snapped, pleased at the man's manner. "You have an acumen about you that matches that of the most levelheaded businessman in London. The business is the better for your association with it." He got to his feet and extended a hand. "I must take my leave. If you are certain there is nothing more I can do to alleviate the force of my grandmother's words, I will wish you a pleasant night and be on my way."

Ashley grasped the hand and bowed slightly. "You have already done more than necessary, sir. I thank you for venturing forth this night to me. It

53

instills in me a feeling of security to know you concern yourself in such a manner."

"Yes," Brinsley said, moving toward the door, "of course. You are a valuable portion of the business, Ashley, and as such you deserve better than you received this night. Until tomorrow, then. A pleasant good night."

"And the same to you, sir," Currante answered, holding the door open until his employer was out and on his way down the steps. When Brinsley had passed from sight, he shut the door with force, his eyes glittering, his mouth drawn into a grimace. "And take yourself and your ancient and foolish grandmother and choke on it, sir," he snarled. Then, an oath on his lips concerning the lack of justice in the world, he donned a light coat and stepped from the room.

Some thirty minutes later Ashley Currante entered a dimly lit café and made his way past the service section to a short flight of stairs. Moments later he stopped at the first of several doors and stepped into a room done in red and yellow to face a painted-faced woman, who sat at a cheap dressing table.

"You're late," said the woman, without looking up from her ministrations in front of the mirror.

"I am never late," answered Currante, removing his coat and crossing the room to place his lips

54

against the nape of her neck. "Must you use such a wealth of that infernal stuff?"

She shrugged and met his eyes in the reflection of the mirror. "The profits reaped here are due to that infernal stuff. I shall one day tire of waiting for you as I have tonight. There will come a time when this room will be empty when you open the door."

His eyes narrowed momentarily. Then, without warning, he swung an open hand and slapped her harshly from behind. She fell from the bench to the floor under the impact of the blow. A sound of pain escaped her lips as she landed roughly on the oaken surface.

"You bastard," she exclaimed, hatred gleaming from her eyes.

He stood over her, his fist doubled in a threatening ball. His black eyes seemed to warn of an unseen evil within their master. "Hold your tongue, whore," he commanded, "lest I make short work of you. I will stand for no harsh treatment this night."

She cringed at the acid in his voice. Then, when she thought he would again hit her, he reached to take her hand and lift her to her feet.

"Now," he said, "enough of your antics. Remove your dressing gown and prepare for me. I shall go for wine and return shortly." With that he stepped from the room and made his way to the café below.

Behind him the woman gritted her teeth and cupped a hand over the spot where his fist had struck. "Bastard," she growled. She removed her garb and made her way to the waiting bed.

CHAPTER FIVE

The first rays of a new day's sun pushed their way into Melissa's bedroom and fell across the sleeping girl's face. The warmth penetrated to her sleeping mind and only minutes later she opened her eyes and stretched herself awake. After surrendering to a long yawn, she rose from the bed and crossed to a basin to wash the last vestiges of sleep from her eyes. Her thoughts turned to the preceding evening, and she smiled. "Grandmother," she said aloud, the smile broadening.

She donned a robe and hurriedly made her way down the stairs to the kitchen, a plan of surprise in mind.

The cook and servants looked up as she entered the room. A maid some years older than Melissa smiled a greeting to her and asked, "And what is it you are in such a rush about this fine morning, lass? You seem to have the devil riding your behind."

Melissa laughed. "I would have breakfast taken to my grandmother's room at the first indication that she stirs. Her travel here was demanding, and I would let her know she is welcome."

A short burst of laughter from all present met

the statement. The maid shook her head slightly and said, "Why Melissa, child, the duchess was about before the new day found itself. She ate more than an hour ago and is, even now, in the parlor scanning yesterday's post and mouthing harsh statements concerning those who sleep their lives away to no avail."

This information sent Melissa into fresh peals of laughter. Finally she turned to the servants. "I would breakfast in the parlor then," she said. "I shall attempt to convince my grandmother that not everyone who sleeps until day's light is a laggard." She was still chuckling when she stepped from the kitchen and made her way toward the front of the house.

Upon the girl's extrance into the parlor, the old lady looked up from her paper. Studying the robe, she asked, "Is this the manner in which you plan to attend the day's business, Missy?"

A smile on her face, Melissa crossed to kiss the woman's cheek. Straightening, she answered, "There are few in this world who can regain the strength of one lost day in the few hours you spend abed, Grandmother. I rose from my bed with intentions of surprising you by having your morning meal served in your room. The servants found my suggestion humorous."

"Hummph!" was the retort. "And it is little they have to laugh about. I sat waiting when the first of them entered the kitchen to begin the day.

There are none in this house who make use of the time alloted by God. Ah, well, I suppose such a thing is referred to as progress."

Taking a seat beside the old woman, Melissa frowned slightly in thought. Finally she asked, "Is there proper time for you to explain the meaning of your words last evening, Grandmother?"

"My words concerning what, child?"

"Concerning the reason for your unannounced visit at this particular time. Though I am more than pleased to have you here, it does seem passing strange that none knew of your coming."

The woman nodded. "Very well, Missy, I will tell you of my reason, though you must not speak of it where other ears might hear. There are plenty of people who swear I am becoming light of weight in the head. I would not have more thinking the same."

The seriousness of her tone made an impression on the girl. "You have my promise that it will go no further, Grandmother. Tell me."

"It was a dream, child," the duchess said matter-of-factly. "No, don't laugh at the idea. It is not the first occasion when such a thing has driven me to the side of one for whom I care. I was but two days into a holiday at Brighton when such a dream occurred, indicating that the old duke was in need of my presence. He was stricken only hours after I reached his side."

Melissa sat silently, staring at the old woman for

59

a long moment. Then with a nod of acceptance she said, "I believe you, Grandmother. Though it is indeed passing strange that such a thing should occur, I have heard of others who have been so affected. But I cannot fancy what reason there could be for you to be summoned here at this time."

"Nor can I," the woman answered. "But summoned I was. I have an inkling of the reason, but I will withhold judgment until I am certain." She hesitated a moment before adding, "I must go to the city today. There is a person there with whom I would speak."

Realizing she had received all the explanation the duchess intended to give for her visit, Melissa got to her feet, saying, "Then I shall accompany you. Even now my meal is being prepared. I have asked that it be served in here."

"I shall sit with you while you dine," her grandmother told her. "However, the visit to the city I must make alone. We shall go together another time to view the shops."

A conspiratorial smile took the girl's lips. "Secrets at your age, Grandmother? Tell me, is it a gentleman friend you intend to visit?"

A slight tic pulled at the old lips. The green eyes sparkled momentarily, and she said, "I would certainly hope such is the case. It is, however, no business of yours. Remember your place and show respect to one who shares responsibility for your being here."

Thirty minutes later, after a pleasant breakfast chat with the old lady, Melissa stood in the doorway and watched the ancient carriage leave the drive and head toward the center of London. She still stood thus when a sound from behind caught her attention. Turning, she faced her father as he made his way down the stairs.

"You are about early, Melissa," he said, a question in his glance. "Why do you stand in the doorway? Is something amiss?"

"Nothing, Father," she answered with a shake of her head. "I simply watched Grandmother on her way."

"Grandmother? On her way to where? Good Lord, it is barely seven o'clock."

Melissa shrugged. "She insisted it was necessary to visit the city. I did not feel it in me to question her motives."

He nodded with a grimace. "You are wise to come to such a decision, child. Should she feel you were prying, there's no telling what she might do. Blast! I feel my morning meal will be tasteless."

"Father!" Melissa exclaimed. "Grandmother cares for all of us. For you to say such a thing is unlike you."

"I realize that, child. You do not, however, realize the sensitivity of my stomach where your

61

grandmother is concerned. For some reason she takes drastic toll on my digestion." He shook his head in despair. "To the city at such an hour. I do believe the woman is slipping her mind." Still mumbling to himself, he turned from his daughter and made his way to the dining room. Behind him she closed the door and, with a smile of sympathy for her father, made her way back to her room to dress for the day.

At approximately the same moment that Melissa had stepped from her bed in Brinsley House, Ashley Currante awoke and left the warmth of the woman's body who lay beside him. Donning his clothing, he reached to shake her awake. "Come, woman," he snarled, "the day has begun. I would have a report of our venture. Tell me, has the vacant room been filled?"

"The day before yesterday," she answered, rubbing her eyes. She sat up in the bed, allowing the covers to fall and expose her bare breasts. "A child from the country. She arrived and was obviously alone in the city. She was quite grateful to have one such as myself befriend her. Though she has accepted two men, she is, of necessity, still under the drugs. She will come to accept her lot soon, however. She is but in her sixteenth year."

Instant anger filled the man's face. "Why did you not speak of this last night, woman?"

She met the angry glance and smiled bitterly.

"So that you might share her bed rather than mine, Ashley? It had been all of two weeks since I've seen you. The girl will be here the next time you call. By that time she will be all willingness—a much more suitable bed partner for her employer."

"One day your humor will cost you," he warned. "I hunger. Though I doubt there is decent food in the sty below, I will attempt to fill my needs. I shall expect the young one to be waiting for me in a fortnight." Turning, he left the room and made his way down the stairs to the café kitchen.

"Ah, Mr. Currante," a grizzled man said from his place at a table when Ashley entered the kitchen. "And how was your night, sir?"

"Satisfactory," Currante answered. "Is there anything worth putting in one's mouth?"

Getting to his feet, the café manager said, "The pork is passable, sir. The beef, on the other hand, is at the point of turning. I fear we shall take a loss on that."

"Loss?" Currante exclaimed. "Are you mad? Profit is not made by taking losses. Boil the accursed beef half again as long and add spices. None will know the difference." His irritation plain, he crossed to seat himself at the table. "I would have the records. And the food I asked of may be forgotten. I shall breakfast elsewhere."

"Aye, sir" was the answer. Minutes later the

representative was studying the figures in a thick journal.

After some twenty minutes of perusing the records he closed the book and handed it back to the waiting café manager. "The bounty, then, dolt," he snapped, "and pray you it is not short."

Half an hour later he stepped from the café, sent a glance in both directions, and returned to his meager rooms. A smile of satisfaction wreathed his face as he walked.

CHAPTER SIX

It was nearing eight o'clock when the duchess's carriage drew to a stop at the front stoop of a well-appointed town house in a wealthy section of London. Instantly the driver was off his seat and at the door to attend his mistress. She stepped from the carriage with a word to him concerning the time she would be. Then she was up the steps, lifting the knocker.

Only moments after her summons the door was opened by a liveried butler. He looked first directly in front of him, then tilted his head back so that he might look into the face of the woman who had rapped at such an early hour.

"Yes, milady?" he asked, studying the regal face.

"I would speak with the earl," she answered the query.

For a moment it seemed he would turn her away, then his glance left her and settled on the coat of arms that shone in golden splendor on the door of the waiting carriage. His glance returned to her face. "And whom shall I say is calling, madam?" he asked.

"Tell him Carrie awaits the opportunity to relieve him of another forty pounds at the card table. That will be sufficient."

"Ma'am? I hardly think—"

"That is obvious," she snapped, her tone hardening. "Do as I say else Charlie will have your ears for his lunch."

The butler reddened, but wisely made no further protest. "I shall give him the message," he said, stepping back as if to close the door.

She stepped forward, pushing the door full open as she entered the house. The green eyes filled with fire, and it was that fire that turned the butler instantly and sent him toward the innards of the house. Moments later the fire in those old eyes died as a roar of pleasure came from the direction the butler had gone.

"Carrie!" came the loud exclamation. "Carrie, here?" A tall, handsome man of some sixty years stepped into the hallway and moved quickly toward the duchess, his arms outstretched in greeting. "Duchess," he exclaimed. "Whatever are you doing waking the dead at this hour? No matter. It is so good to see you again." He had hold of her hands and was bowing over them. When he straightened, he met her eyes and asked, "Could it be that you have reconsidered my offer of marriage?"

She laughed outright at the question. "Hardly, you ancient rake. What use would I have for one who is so young as to be inept at gaming. It is good to see you again, Charlie. I assume you are well."

"Much better at this moment than I was before your arrival, Carrie. Come. Breakfast with me." He led her down the hall toward a splendid dining room, where two maids and the butler stood waiting.

"I've eaten," she informed him. "I will take tea, though, if it is hot."

"And if it isn't, we shall see that it is made so," her host answered, motioning to the servants. "Set a place for the duchess," he ordered, adding to the butler, "And, Truman, remove that silly expression from your face. You appear to have seen a ghost."

The butler bowed to the duchess, saying, "My apologies, your Grace. I did not know—"

"What?" the earl demanded, his attention going to the woman. "Has something happened?"

"Hush, Charles," she said. With a nod to the butler she continued, "Your man and I had a moment's discussion at the door. It is none of your affair if I wish to make advances toward your servants. I recall a time when such a thing would have surprised you not at all."

Though he smiled at the answer, his eyes were on the butler, a question in them.

The manservant cleared his throat. "Her Grace is too kind, milord. I fear I, in spite of the obvious indication of the crest on the carriage door, did not take her for a duchess." He dropped his glance

67

with the admission and stood silently, awaiting the earl's wrath.

"Good Lord, Truman," the earl laughed, "I have underestimated your courage. It is no wonder you wore such a stricken look when you announced her. I am surprised you could speak at all." He turned to the duchess, who stood smiling at the statement. "You have in all likelihood put Truman's nerves on razor's edge for the next week. I fear a beggar could rap at my door and gain entrance at this moment. Come, Carrie. Sit down."

"It was a mistake anyone could have made," she answered, taking a seat. "Don't assail him with it."

"Assail him with it?" the earl laughed. "I doubt that anything I could say would surpass what I'm certain he received from you, Carrie. Now, tell me, why do you storm my house at such an hour?"

She hesitated only briefly. "I have had another of my dreams, Charles. It has taken me to Brinsley House. I feel there is evil afoot involving my people."

He nodded in understanding. "In the forty years I have known and loved you, there has never been any reason to question these dreams of yours. What is it you wish of me?"

"First," she said with a smile, "that you gain twenty years of age that I might test your true intentions with such endearing statements. Second, are you yet involved in that rotten business of prying into the private affairs of others?"

He smiled broadly, then broke into laughter. "Ah, Carrie mine, you refuse, as always, to believe there can be such a thing as a private investigation that does not edge on the indiscreet. Yes, I am still a portion of the business, though for several years now I have had excellent men managing in my stead. What is it you wish?"

"I would have information concerning two men. The first I wish to meet this day if possible. The other I will require full particulars concerning. Can it be done—discreetly?"

"Of course," he answered, lifting a table bell to call the butler. "The one for today must be seen to instantly if you are to have time to meet him." He turned his attention to the butler, saying, "Send a message to James Parkins. He is to attend me at the earliest possible moment."

When the butler had hurried away to obey the order, the duchess reached to cover the earl's hand with her own. "Thank you, Charles. It cheers one to realize there are such friends as you. I will see that you are amply paid."

"You border on the insolent, Carrie—though that in itself is not surprising. Years ago you paid for any service I could render." A chuckle escaped him suddenly, and his eyes lit up. "Do you recall the moment when both you and I were called to a private audience with the queen?"

She threw back her head and laughed heartily at the reminder of an occasion thirty years earlier. "She was taken aback with the both of us, was she not?"

"With you, more than me," he answered. "Till, her dying day I think she did not actually believe that you, being a lady in your fifty-third year, had actually questioned the legitimacy of Lord Hambright's birth to his face. And had it not been for the one-hundred-odd persons present at the occasion, I doubt that any in the kingdom would have thought it of you." He suddenly lost control of himself and burst into laughter.

"And your statement in my defense concerning your investigations were equally unbelievable to her, though they proved without doubt that I was correct in calling the fool an old bastard." She, too, broke into laughter, and they sat as good friends, enjoying memories of their younger days.

It was nearing the noon hour when the duchess bade good-bye to her friend and stepped into the carriage. As the wheels were put into motion, she leaned from the window and again called her thanks to the earl for his assistance. Then, settling back against the cushions, she contemplated what she had learned from the investigation.

She was still deep in thought when the carriage drew to a stop and the driver opened the door to announce, "The Red Boar Inn, your Grace. Shall I accompany you?"

"That will not be necessary," she answered. "Secure the horses and use the time as you will. I would suggest you partake of food. I may be longer than supposed." With that she crossed the walk and entered the inn.

To her relief the inn was nearly empty. Only two of the open tables were occupied. From behind the bar, a man who bore the look of an innkeeper made his way toward her. "Ah, Duchess," he greeted her with a slight bow. "And how is it we of this establishment can be of service to you?"

"You are acquainted with me, sir?" she asked, the green eyes questioning him.

"Only from afar and many years ago, milady. I was but a young man when your husband, the duke, paid me handsomely for merely holding his steed and yours. You do appear as commanding now as you did then."

She nodded acceptance of the compliment. "I seek an American, a man by the name of Brett Boyden. I am informed he relaxes here during this period each day."

"He does, indeed, milady. I will fetch him."

"No," she said. "I will go to him."

"Very well, your Grace, come. I will show you to his table." So saying, he led her through the maze of tables to a row of curtained booths along the far side of the inn. With a motion of his hand he indicated one of the closed booths, asking, "Shall I announce you, milady?"

She shook her head and handed the man a coin. "I shall see to that portion of it, sir. My thanks, not only for your service this day, but for your fond memory and excellent manner with the turn of a compliment."

With a bow he left her. Turning, she waited until he was well on his way back to his position behind the bar before pulling the curtain back to face the man within the booth. Instantly the green eyes took in the open-collared shirt, the not unhandsome face, and the gray questioning eyes under a rumpled mass of hair.

"Madam?" he asked, his fork poised only inches from his lips.

"I would join you if I might," she said, taking a seat across from him before he could answer. "It is of some importance that we speak."

The gray eyes narrowed slightly. He continued the motion of the fork and proceeded to chew the food as he studied her. Finally, when the bite had been swallowed, he asked, "Have you eaten, my good lady?"

"Food is not important at this moment," she answered. "My reason for seeking you out is."

He shook his head and again forked food into his mouth. "Perhaps you are correct, dear lady. That does not, however, answer my question. Have you eaten?"

A hint of irritation touched her eyes at the repeated question and the man's negligent manner. "I have not," she said finally.

"Then you shall dine with me. Let it never be said that Brett Boyden allowed any lady to hunger in his presence. The beef is excellent. The lamb and pork are acceptable and nothing more." He called to the manager and turned again to her. "What would you like?"

The brashness of the man brought a hint of a smile to her lips. "Since you seem beyond the point of concern as to why I approach you, I shall have the beef."

"Excellent choice," he smiled. "Would you like tea?"

"What is it you drink, sir?" she asked as the manager of the inn neared the booth.

"Ale is my drink, milady, but I understand the tea in this establishment is without peer."

"And the quality of their ale?"

He lifted his mug and drank deeply before saying, "Excellent. I can attest to that."

Fixing him with a calculating glance, she asked, "Are you besot with this drink, sir? It is uncommon to find one who partakes of ale or any other strong drink before the midday hour."

He chuckled lightly. "As to the habit you mention, no. I will not have a habit which controls me. As to the difficulty of finding those who drink before the noontime, I fear you are mistaken. One has but to peer into the private lives of others to find many who do so, unless I am in error."

She again put her studious glance on him and nodded slightly when he ignored her to return to his eating. "I believe I, too, shall have a tankard of the ale," she said when he had completed filling his mouth.

A dancing light entered the gray eyes. Turning to the openmouthed innkeeper, he swallowed and ordered, "Bring the lady a large ale and the beef."

It seemed for a moment that the man would protest, but with a shrug he turned and left the booth.

"The innkeeper appears astonished at your choice of beverage, milady," Boyden said, stabbing a piece of beef with his fork. "Are you known in this establishment?"

"To a degree. Why do you ask?"

Placing the beef in his mouth, he shrugged. When the meat had been consumed, he said, "I take it from the innkeeper's expression that you are someone of importance. True?"

She laughed shortly. "And would it make a difference in your manner if I were the queen, sir?"

"Hardly. I have no knowledge of being in the queen's or any other's debt."

She was silent for a moment, then with a motion toward his bowl of food, she said, "Gentlemen of England would await the coming of the lady's food before proceeding with their own meal."

74

"And in the process end up eating cold food," he retorted. "I don't recall inviting you to intrude on my meal, madam. I, therefore, feel no compunction to suffer from your coming. Since you seem aware of my name, would it be possible for me to know yours?"

"I believe you may call me Carrie. And, if it should happen that we become friends, there is another I would have you meet who has the same privilege."

"Very well then, Carrie." His eyes narrowed suddenly. "Since we are acquainted to a degree, what is there about the Brinsley lass you would discuss with me?"

For the first time in many years, the duchess found herself taken aback. She was silent for several moments before asking, "Brinsley? What brings you to think I am here to discuss any of the name of Brinsley?"

He leaned back and wiped his mouth with a napkin. Suddenly, his lips split into a broad smile and a chuckle escaped them. He lifted his tankard and drank deeply. "Take away—let me see—yes, take away sixty or so years, and you could have been the one I approached yesterday afternoon at the demonstration of some machine or other. You are of an age to surpass most so I would judge you to be the girl's great-grandmother."

The innkeeper arrived at that moment with her order. Placing it on the table, he sent a look of disparagement at Boyden, bowed to the duchess, and said, "If you have need of anything else, you have only to call, your Grace."

She waved him away with a hand and, when the curtain was again in place, spoke to Boyden. "You are very discerning, sir. You have called me right. I am pleased to know that Missy matches me to such a degree."

"Missy Brinsley, is it?"

"Melissa is her name. And you are Brett Boyden, a relative of one Seth Boyden, who—unless I am mistaken—gave America the shiny material we call patent leather."

He nodded without a change of expression. "An uncle." He paused, allowing a smile to pull at the corner of his mouth. "The innkeeper referred to you as your Grace. Am I to understand that you are titled?"

"A duchess," she said shortly with a negligent wave of her hand. "To you I am Carrie. Now, unless I misguess, the name Brett Boyden should also be that of your father. It was he, I suppose, who your President Monroe called upon for service in the forming of several new American states in the last few years."

He shook his head. "No, Duchess. Both my mother and father met their deaths some twenty years ago. Jim did me the honor of asking my advice on the instances you refer to."

She sat in silence for some time before nodding.

"I should have known. And you will not refer to me as duchess a second time, Brett. Whether you will have it so or not, I feel you and I are to become friends."

"Very well, Carrie, but you should eat your meal before it cools." As she began eating he added, "I will admit to having suffered less appealing ladies in my time. It would come as no surprise if you should best the lot of them at anything you attempt. Tell me, why have you sought me out?"

"To invite you to visit me at Brinsley House this evening for dinner."

His laugh had a touch of acid in it. "You are, I fear, not aware of the facts, Carrie. The gentleman, Brinsley—father of your great-granddaughter—has made his opinion of me quite clear. He would in no way accept my presence in his house."

She snorted derisively. "I did not ask you to visit my grandson, sir."

"What purpose could a visit from me serve? It would do nothing but further irritate an already irate father."

"It would serve to allow me further knowledge of a man whose memory brings a light to the eye of my favorite great-granddaughter. The girl is dear to me in a special way." She ceased speaking long enough to take a bite of the food and a drink of the ale. Then, "You approached her and rendered a compliment, I understand. Was the compliment an honest one?"

"I would not have given it had it not been," he answered. "Where, pray tell, is this leading us?"

"You found Melissa attractive?"

He nodded. "Very attractive. There is something about her demeanor that leads me to believe that she is of a character much the same as—"

"Yes? Much the same as what?" she asked.

He chuckled. "I was about to say much the same as my own. I would recall that and add that her character is similar to yours as well as mine. Duchess Carrie, has there been a moment in your short life when the opinions of others have controlled you?"

"Never!" she snorted. "I, sir, am my own person and shall remain so until my death. Tell me. Since Melissa is of a height besting six feet, do you not find that a deterrent to your attraction for her? You can be no more than within two inches of her."

A puzzled expression took his features. "I had not planned on an exchange of clothing with her nor her with me, Carrie. Of what difference is height?"

"Hah!" the duchess exploded. "Well said. You will call this very evening to dine with me. Arrive at the hour of seven." She tipped the mug to finish the ale and then, sighing heavily, got up from the booth saying, "Excellent. I shall expect you."

Boyden reached to touch her wrist. "Hold, Carrie. Though I respect you and find myself taken with your ways, I cannot promise to attend you this evening. There are plans that have been made for some days."

Reaching to lay her free hand atop his, she looked him directly in the eye. "Plans, as I recall, were made to be changed, Brett. I would consider it a favor should you rap at the door of Brinsley House at seven. My thanks for the meal and the ale. It was delightful." With that she pulled from his grasp and left.

For some five minutes after her departure, he sat in deep thought. Then, a smile on his features, he shrugged and said aloud, "If this Melissa is half the woman that one is, the time will be well spent." He completed his meal and left the inn.

CHAPTER SEVEN

Two minutes before the hour of seven Brett Boyden checked his watch in the light of two wall-hung lamps at the Brinsley stoop. With an appreciative glance around the property, he chuckled to himself prior to raising the knocker. *Well, if I am to be bodily ejected, at least I shall come to rest on well-kept grounds*, he thought. He dropped the knocker and waited until the door was opened by a tall, rigid-backed butler.

"Yes, sir?" the servant asked, peering down his nose at Boyden.

"Brett Boyden calling upon the duchess," the American answered, amused at the haughty manner of the man.

With obvious reluctance the servant stepped back, saying, "If you will wait here, sir, I shall inquire of the duchess as to her receiving of guests." Turning away, he vanished into the bowels of Brinsley House.

Reginald Brinsley looked up when the butler entered the room. His manner was irate when he asked, "Well, what is it, man? Is something amiss?"

The butler bowed slightly. "No, sir. It is a caller who asks for the duchess. A Mr. Boyden."

"Boyden? Boyden?" Brinsley demanded in disbelief. "What in thunder can the man want here? Tell him he is—"

"Tell him he is to enter and join us," the duchess said from across the parlor. "I mentioned a guest would be dining with us at my request this night, Reginald. He is here."

Turning to her, Brinsley stared wide-eyed. "You invited the oaf into my home, Grandmother? I will not have it." He turned back to the butler. "Tell the man there has been a mistake. He is to leave at once."

The butler turned to leave but was stopped by the duchess's command to halt. He turned and faced her, looking as one should look when caught between two such forces as those.

"Ask Mr. Boyden to wait," she ordered. "I shall get a wrap and join him." She sighed slightly and added, "I must visit the old duke's solicitors tomorrow. There is much that needs examination."

The butler nodded and again turned to leave, only to be stopped in his tracks by Brinsley's call. Turning to his employer, he said, "Yes, Sir Reginald?"

Shaken by the duchess's veiled threat, Brinsley sent a quick glance at his wife and ordered, "Show the infernal man in. And for heaven's sake, send someone to locate my daughter."

When the butler had gone, the duchess again sank to her chair, saying, "I appreciate your allowing my friend to dine with us, Reginald. There are few grandsons in this world who care so for their grandmothers."

Exasperation swept over Brinsley's features. Teeth gritted, he faced his wife, demanding, "Where is our daughter? Doesn't she receive information concerning the time of the evening meal in this house?"

"Now, Reginald," Lady Brinsley began, "there is nothing—"

The butler returned at that moment with Brett Boyden. Upon his announcement of the visitor, he turned immediately and made his way to the kitchen to send a maid for Melissa.

"Ah, Brett," the duchess said happily, getting to her feet. "Come, I would like for you to meet my grandson and his wife. Reginald, Edith, this gentleman is from the United States of America. Mr. Brett Boyden."

For an instant it seemed Brinsley would refuse the hand extended by Boyden. Then, catching the glint in his grandmother's green eyes, he swallowed hard and got to his feet, saying, "Mr. Boyden, I believe we met earlier."

"But not properly, sir," Boyden said with a bow. When Brinsley released his hand, he turned to Lady Brinsley saying, "Milady, I thank you for allowing such a one as I to be guest in your home.

It is a rare occasion in this country when I am fortunate enough to dine anywhere but at the inn."

Lady Brinsley found herself at a loss for words. Nodding in answer to the remarks, she sent a nervous glance at her husband, a plea in her eyes.

Melissa swept into the room at that moment. Her gown of soft pink and white lace brought out the luster of her hair and the glint of her green eyes. She stopped short when her glance fell on Brett Boyden. "I . . ." she began, then moved forward to offer her hand to him. "Mr. Boyden, I believe," she said, looking down into his gray eyes. "I had not planned on seeing you again."

His lips pulled into a smile as he accepted her hand and bent over it. "I had the pleasure of meeting Carrie today. It was at her invitation that I called."

The girl's glance swung to her grandmother, and an expression of gratitude tinged with devilment took her face. Returning her attention to Boyden, she was about to speak, when his left eye closed in a wink.

"You are, if anything, more lovely now than on our first meeting, Missy," he said before she could speak.

"Hummph!" Brinsley coughed noisily. "Well, dinner is waiting. Shall we proceed to the dining room?"

Boyden turned to the duchess, asking, "May I have your arm, Carrie?"

"Or me, yours," the duchess amended, stepping to his side.

Then, his glance going to Melissa, he said, "And I would be all but blessed if I were allowed to attend you to the dining room also, Missy."

The old woman's eyes met the young girl's, and a message passed between the two. Melissa smiled at Boyden, saying, "It would be my pleasure, sir."

With a tall lady on each arm, Boyden faced a florid-complected Brinsley. "Sir, you must agree I am a fortunate man to have two of England's loveliest ladies as dinner partners this evening," Boyden commented.

It seemed Brinsley would shatter his teeth, they clenched so tightly. Finally he nodded and took his wife's arm. "Quite so, sir," he got out as he stepped smartly from the parlor toward the dining room.

Melissa met her great-grandmother's eyes over their escort's head. "Grandmother," she said, a smile of impishness on her lips, "you should have warned me. Father is—"

"—a total ass," the duchess finished for her. Then to Boyden she said, "My great-granddaughter is quite taken with you, Brett. Her taste in men rivals my own. And a good thing, I must say."

"Grandmother!" Melissa gasped as Boyden broke into laughter and led them after the Brinsleys. "I—I—Mr. Boyden, I certainly do not—"

"—lie as a general rule," the duchess chuckled. "Ah, well, the young will play their games. I do hope the food is palatable this evening, Brett."

Boyden was nearing the bursting point with chuckling. Shaking his head, he looked up into the girl's eyes, saying, "Carrie and I found ourselves taken with each other at once. I fear it stems from the fact that neither of us care to disguise our words or conceal our feelings. I further fear she has caused a situation of discomfort by inviting me. If you prefer, I will take my leave."

Melissa saw that the laughter and glow of candor had left his gray eyes. She realized suddenly that she felt at ease on this man's arm, as she had never felt with another. Her eyes again met those of the duchess and she knew in that instant what she would do.

With a slight nod of her head she said, "Mr. Boyden, I would not hear of your leaving. Though I am certain my cheeks redden, I am not, as Grandmother has pointed out, a liar. I would very much enjoy having you beside me for the meal."

"And afterward," the duchess put in, "I would appreciate Brett's company on a walk through the gardens."

The sparkle returned to his smile and his eyes. "I shall be happy to attend both wishes, ladies." Then they were in the dining room.

When they were seated, with Melissa at the right hand of the visitor and the duchess directly across from him, Brinsley asked, "And, Boyden, how is it you come to know my grandmother?"

"An act of fate," Boyden answered. "It seems, though, that I've known Carrie since the beginning of time."

Lady Brinsley lifted her wineglass and sipped noisily. In a tremulous voice she said, "Not even Reginald is allowed to call the duchess by Carrie, Mr. Boyden. You must, in truth, be a close friend of hers."

Her husband's expression silenced her. She stared at her plate.

"Brett is the finest of friends," the duchess said ignoring her grandson's bitter look. "I cherish him for his manners and his outlook on life."

Melissa turned to Boyden. "And what brings you to London, Mr. Boyden?"

"Brett, if you will, Missy. I am here on holiday, nothing more. I must admit that until this moment the holiday spirit had evaded me totally."

"And what do you occupy yourself with in the Colonies, sir?" Brinsley demanded in a tone that left little doubt as to his feelings for the American.

Boyden hesitated while servants placed plates of food before them. With a smile he said, "I am, for the most part, an adventurer, sir. There is much in America that calls to men and women of spirit. I find it difficult to resist the urge to explore the unknown country to the west of the States."

Brinsley's eyes widened at the word "adventurer." His glance swung to his grandmother, as if damning the woman for inflicting such a person upon them.

"Emissary would serve as a better description, would it not, Brett?" the duchess asked without taking her eyes from the food before her. "It was your signature on the joint-control treaty between Britain and America for the region called Oregon, was it not?"

He nodded, a smile tugging his lips. "In eighteen eighteen, Carrie. You seem well versed on the happenings of my country."

The knowledge did little to reduce the irritation visible in Brinsley's face. He did, however, ask, "You acted as emissary for— What is he called?"

"The President?" Boyden asked. "Yes. Jim requested that I be present. Mine was not the only signature on the treaty, however. There were others there who were, and still are, instrumental in my country's future."

The information silenced Brinsley for a moment. During the lull in the interrogation, the duchess met her great-granddaughter's eyes and smiled. "The food is excellent, is it not?" she asked of all present.

"Excellent," Melissa agreed with a smile. "Have you never made a visit to England before, Brett?"

He nodded. "Several times. I have not, however, enjoyed myself as I do now."

"The food cools," the duchess snapped. "No one enjoys cold food. If there are more questions this family can ask to pry into Brett's life, they shall wait until we have completed the meal." She fell to eating without another word. After a moment Brinsley sighed and then he, too, attacked the food.

When dessert had been finished, Brinsley stood, pushing back his chair. "Well, Boyden, we realize you must have plans for the evening. Do not allow us to keep you from them."

"Nonsense!" the duchess snapped before Boyden could answer. "Brett has promised to accompany me on a tour of the gardens. I would have him see the care extended to everything at Brinsley House." She got to her feet, her eyes held fast on the American's. "The meal will settle easier with a walk, I believe."

He nodded, an ill-concealed smile on his lips. "It would be my pleasure, Carrie."

The butler entered the room at that moment to announce that Mr. Ashley Currante awaited the presence of Sir Reginald in the library.

"Blast!" Brinsley exclaimed, throwing his napkin to the plate. "Now what can the matter be?" With a glance of frustration at his grandmother, he stepped past Boyden and made his way from the room.

Upon his leaving, the duchess asked, "And,

Missy, would you care to enjoy the night air with Brett and myself?"

Lady Brinsley's head came up. She opened her mouth to speak, hesitated, and finally said, "I don't believe Reginald would permit such a thing, your Grace."

"Oh, tish and piffle," the duchess said, "and stop calling me your Grace. I am Grandmother to all in this house. Well, Missy?"

Nodding, Melissa said, "I would be pleased to chaperon you and Brett, Grandmother. Let me get our wraps." She hurried from the room without looking in her mother's direction and returned only moments later to hand the duchess a shawl.

"Very well, then," the old woman said, "let us go to the gardens. Unless I mistake it, they are lovely in the moonlight." Taking Boyden's arm, she led him from the room with Melissa trailing only steps behind.

Brinsley entered the library, extremely angry at his grandmother and the Colonist who had forced himself upon them. He faced his representative, asking, "Well, what is it, Ashley? It seems an odd hour for you to call on business matters."

A puzzled expression crossed Currante's face at his employer's manner. "I'm sorry if I've come at an inconvenient moment, sir. It is, indeed, a matter of business, but I suppose it can wait until tomorrow."

"Oh, good God," Brinsley snorted. "That grandmother of mine has me snapping at all who put themselves before me. Sit down, man. And forgive my anger. If not for that accursed Colonist, I would not be in such a way."

"Colonist, Sir Reginald? You refer to the Boyden dolt?"

"I do, indeed," Brinsley answered with a sigh. "He has this evening, at an invitation from my grandmother, taken the evening meal at my table. Ah, what I would not give to be free of that woman's ways." He stomped to position behind his desk and dropped into the chair. "Even now the two of them are taking a turn of the gardens. I swear, the woman is becoming loose in the head. Well, what is it, Ashley?"

Ashley sat quietly for a long moment, as if in deep thought. Then suddenly he jerked to attention, saying, "Having nothing better to do this evening, I remained at the business to study the books and entries for the last few months, sir. I have found obvious errors."

"Errors?" Brinsley demanded, his interest heightening.

"Yes, sir," Ashley assured him. "Errors that I feel were deliberate. Though I am not certain of my words, it would seem that several hundred pounds—if not more—have been misplaced."

"Misplaced?" Brinsley nearly screamed, coming

to his feet. "Misplaced? How could such a thing happen?"

Currante grimaced at the question. "I have taken notice of but a few entries made before you were required to deal with Mr. Wright, our former bookkeeper. Judging from the few entries I have studied previous to his leaving your employ, I believe several monies have been diverted into accounts that have no bearing in actuality."

Brinsley stood for a moment, groping for words. Finally he burst out, "What are you saying, Ashley?"

Currante shrugged. "Though, as I say, I am not certain, sir, it appears that Wright did partake of several sums of money before leaving us. Had I not been acting in his stead these past days, the fact could easily have gone unnoticed."

"Good God! The money for the walk-along rights as well as other debts will be due within a week. What is the total amount missing?"

"I do not know, sir," Currante answered. "As I have said, I have only studied a few pages of entries. But within those few pages it seems that several hundred pounds have been misplaced."

"Stolen!" Brinsley roared. "Return to the business, Ashley, and study the books. We must know the true state of our finances and we must know immediately. Hurry, man."

Currante pulled a watch from his pocket and

glanced at it. "It is past the hour of eight, sir. I have not supped. It would be—"

"Nonsense, man," Brinsley interrupted. "You will be well paid for this night's work. Go. We must know our true state by morning."

Reluctantly, it seemed, Currante nodded. "Very well, sir, I shall do my utmost to have a report prepared by the morning." Turning, he stepped from the library and made his way from the house. Behind him Brinsley stood as if in shock, his eyes fastened to the open doorway, his fist pressed to his mouth.

"It cannot be," he muttered. "It was going so well. It cannot be."

A broad smile split the representative's face as he gave the carriage driver the address of his rooms. He chuckled lightly as he thought of the next necessary move. "A pity," he said to the night air.

CHAPTER EIGHT

The moon shed its velvet whiteness over the gardens in a cloak of majesty. Boyden, walking between the two women, said, "Such a night as this reminds me of America. It is beautiful."

"And tiring to one such as I," the duchess answered, looking straight ahead. "There is, as I recall, a garden seat just ahead. I believe I shall rest there."

Melissa stopped and studied her great-grandmother in the moonlight. "Is there something I can get for you, grandmother?" she asked in a tone of concern.

"Nothing," the duchess told her. "Once I am off my feet for a few moments, I shall be as fit as new. You children continue your walk. The gardens are worth seeing to anyone who has not had the pleasure before."

Boyden laughed outright. Then, his eyes coming up to meet Melissa's, he said, "Your grandmother takes the part of matchmaker, Missy. Though I can find no argument with such a thing, I will return you to the house if you wish."

"The truth, girl," the duchess snapped before

Melissa could answer. "You walk on the arm of a man, so let your lips speak your true desires."

Melissa was glad for the lack of light. She felt the color of embarrassment flood over her face for a moment, then, when silence had held the three of them for some time, she said, "Very well, Grandmother, the truth without qualm. Yes, Mr. Boyden, I will walk with you. And, sir, you are correct. Grandmother does at this moment fancy herself a matchmaker." She averted her eyes then and added, "And I must admit to a certain pleasure that she sees fit to do so."

"Well said," the duchess snorted as they arrived at the bower seat. "Now, use the moments you have to acquaint yourselves with one another. God knows Reginald will see an end to it soon enough when he discovers Brett has taken the both of us."

"My thanks, Carrie," Boyden said, taking the girl's arm and leading her along the path away from the duchess. When they were out of earshot of the older woman, he met Melissa's eyes, saying, "I had not hoped for such a thing when I lifted the knocker at your door this evening, Missy."

She swallowed and turned from his glance. "Grandmother, though she is my favorite person in all the world, would demand simplicity and truth from all around her." She paused, then added, "I feel I am like her in many ways, Brett.

94

For I have given thought to you many times since our meeting in the glen."

He laughed shortly. "It would have been difficult for you to do otherwise, since my thoughts have been on you constantly since the moment. I feel certain the very air coming to you was filled with my desire to see you again."

She was silent for several steps. Then, as they rounded a corner of the garden path, she stopped and looked into his gray eyes. "Does it not concern you that I best you in height, Brett?" she asked, as if not wishing to hear his answer.

"Concern me?" he asked. "Why should such a thing concern me? As I told Carrie, I have no intention of exchanging clothing with you, nor you with me."

The tension left her with a rush. She stood facing him for a long moment, then his arm moved up to her shoulders and his hand touched the nape of her neck. She felt herself bending slightly and his lips touched hers and held them. Only heartbeats later her arms went around him and her heart soared to the very moon, which set the mood for romance in the Brinsley gardens.

When the embrace broke, she straightened and turned away from him. A moment later, in spite of her efforts to control them, tears came to her eyes and she raised a hand to rub them away.

His touch settled on her arm suddenly. "Melissa love," he whispered in concern, "I'm sorry. I did

95

not intend to take liberties. It is only the night and the moon and your extreme loveliness that have taken my sense of propriety from me. Forgive me, please."

She turned to him, tears sparkling against her cheeks in the moonlight. "Ah, Brett, there is nothing to forgive. Though it make me appear a harlot, your touch has sent me into a world of pleasure." She choked, then laughed. "I must confess that you are the first who has had any desire to commit such an act."

Disbelief was plain on his face. "If it were so, pride in the fact would please me, Melissa. I doubt, however, that there are that many fools in the kingdom."

She shook her head, still wiping at the tears that overflowed her eyelids. "There are none who would do such a thing had I wished it. They concern themselves with the ladies who are of a height more easy to attain than I."

"Then they are, indeed, fools," he told her, drawing her to him a second time. "They are, indeed, fools." Once again he touched her very being and sent her flying into a world of enchantment. It was some moments later when the sound of the duchess's voice came to them, bringing an end to a caress neither wished ended.

"Missy girl," came the whispered call, "your father is in the gardens. Come, the two of you. His anger will be at its peak this moment."

"I care not, Grandmother," Melissa said as they rounded the curve and faced her. "Brett and I have—"

"Of course you have," the duchess said, her expression softening. "This, however, is the time to ease your father's concern. It would be best if Brett could eventually be welcomed to this house. Now, girl, conceal yourself until Brett and I have led your father past this position. Then take yourself to the house and to your room. I shall rap on your door when I go to my quarters."

With a final long look at Boyden, Melissa squeezed his hand and stepped behind a stand of tall bushes.

Instantly the duchess moved to place her arm on the American's, saying, "Very well, Brett, let us continue our walk." Then, in a voice loud enough to be heard some yards away, she said, "And there is the tree planted by my husband when he was but a child."

"Grandmother?" came a call from behind them as Brinsley burst into view along the path.

Pulling to a stop, they turned to face him. When he neared them, he sent a glance first to the older woman, then to the man. Confusion covered his features when he said, "I understood Melissa had accompanied you, Grandmother."

The duchess snorted. "It was her intent, Reginald. However she was taken with a sudden headache. She went to her room to lie down. Is something the matter?"

He hesitated, then shook his head. "Nothing, Grandmother. Forgive me for interrupting your walk." He nodded to Boyden and turned.

"Your gardens are beyond compare, sir," Boyden said. "My thanks for allowing me to view them in the company of your grandmother."

Brinsley turned back to face him. He seemed to search the man's face for signs of humor. Then, finding nothing of such nature there, he nodded. "We are proud of them, sir. Thank you." Then he was gone.

"You have confused him, Brett," the duchess said. "Shame on you. You younger people have no respect for the sensitivities of the aged. Come, it is time I retired to my quarters. I must see to Missy's headache."

Boyden held her arm, bringing her attempt at movement to a stop. He faced her, a smile on his face, for a long moment before gently kissing her cheek. Then he released her, saying, "Would that you were of an age as Melissa, Carrie. Lord, I would be fortunate to take you as my own."

There was no denying the surprise that swept over the old face at the action and the words. She cleared her throat, then with a shake of her head and a chuckle said, "It is my hope your lips found softer sites to attend than they have this moment.

Otherwise I feel it is a broken heart rather than a headache I shall attend. Come, we must return."

"I mean to have her as my wife, Carrie," he said as they stepped along the path. "Make no mistake of that."

She halted and turned back to face him, her manner coldly serious. "The idea is not distasteful to me, Brett. I would suggest, though, that you and Missy both look to your hearts, lest it be you who make the mistake. A moment of stolen passion lacks much as a basis for lasting love. There are many things neither of you know of the other."

He nodded agreement and stepped up beside her to take her arm. "I do not question your wisdom, Carrie. I do, however, maintain a confidence in my own decisions. The stolen moments were enough to tell me that Melissa is the woman I would like to spend the rest of my days beside. I only hope she will come to feel the same toward me."

"That is something only she can decide" was her answer as they entered the house. "Now take yourself to your lodging or to the pub. Get foxed if you must, for many men must do such a thing at times like this."

He chuckled lightly. "The only wine I shall need this night has been taken. The wine of Melissa's lips will render me foxed for a fortnight." He bowed to her at the foot of the staircase and turned to leave the house. Over his shoulder he said softly, "And my thanks to you, Carrie. If there is ever anything a Boyden can do for you, you have but to ask. I am in your debt for life."

She stood watching until he stepped from the house and closed the door behind him. Then, a satisfied smile on her face, she made her way up the stairs and rapped at her great-granddaughter's door.

The portal flew open almost instantly. Melissa stepped forward to take the old woman's hand and draw her into the bedroom. "Oh, Grandmother," she breathed, "never will I be able to thank you for what you have done this night. He is . . . Oh, I cannot find the words to describe him."

"A man, Melissa," the duchess said. "A man by any standards. Are you besot with him?"

Facing her, Melissa blushed slightly, saying, "As no woman has ever been besot by a man before, Grandmother. He kissed me. Twice."

"I would certainly hope as much."

"Oh, but, Grandmother, he cared not that I was of a height above him. His hand went to my neck in a manner so soft I hardly realized that I had bent to meet his lips. And— Oh, the ecstacy of his kisses. Never has anyone been as happy as I."

"Hummph! And on the basis of only two kisses

and as many stolen moments, you feature yourself in love with the man? Are you insane, girl?"

The girl's manner sobered at the harsh question. "I—I thought you liked him, Grandmother. I—" Suddenly, her jawline stiffened. Her shoulders squared and she met the searching glance of the older woman squarely. "Yes, Grandmother, I do feature myself in love with the man. And it is no fleeting thing I feel, either. I love him with all my heart and soul. If ever there is a time when he would suggest such a thing, I shall go with him wherever he asks."

The expression of harshness transformed itself into a broad smile on the old face. "Then, it is as it should be, child. For he, too, has found one he cares for this night. Now take you to your bed and rest. It has been an exciting day for you. I must seek out my grandson and determine what concerns him. When we met in the garden, there was more in his face than the possibility of his daughter being smitten."

"Ah, you cannot mean you will not tell me of Brett's words with you after I'd gone from his presence, Grandmother. The torture of not knowing his feelings will be the death of me by morning, I am certain."

"Nonsense, girl," the duchess laughed. "We spoke not of you but of important things, things such as the tree the old duke planted when he was a child. How conceited of you to think that you were the subject of our discussion."

Melissa suddenly stepped forward and threw her arms about the old woman, a sound of happiness emanating from her lips. "Ah, Grandmother, you tease so. Please, did he indicate a liking for me?"

Pushing the girl away gently, the duchess said, "No, child, not a liking. His indication ran much deeper than that. I cannot and will not tell you his words. Rest assured that your love is not wasted on that one. Take yourself to bed." Turning, she left the room.

As the door closed behind the old woman, Melissa clapped her hands together and spun around with happiness. Over and over she repeated, "He loves me. He loves me."

Brett Boyden settled back against the cushions of the carriage and turned his thoughts to the moments he had spent with Melissa in the Brinsley gardens. A smile held his face at the memory and suddenly he said aloud, "It is true. The good Lord does watch over fools and Boydens. She will be mine if there is a way I can see to it." He began whistling softly, the pleased expression still on his face and the sound on his lips when he paid the driver and made his way to his room.

CHAPTER NINE

"Well, Reginald, what is it?" the duchess demanded, standing across the desk from Brinsley. "And don't attempt to lie. Your expressions have ever given you away when there is trouble. Is it a woman?"

For a moment he attempted to meet the demanding stare, but failed. "It is nothing for you to concern yourself with, Grandmother. It is a business matter."

"The business was turned over to you by the old duke, Reginald. It was placed in your hands for safe keeping. Do not say it is not my concern. I would know what has taken place."

Realizing the futility of arguing further, he said in a low voice, "It appears a former employee may have stolen funds from the business under the guise of false accounts. There is nothing determined yet, but it appears such may be the case."

"How much?"

"Grandmother, I will see to it. Do not concern yourself. Believe me, I—"

"—place your trust in the wrong people as always," she finished for him. "Now, tell me, how much has been stolen?"

"Only a few hundred pounds, I'm certain. It is nothing that cannot be handled by me. It—"

"Only a few hundred pounds? I do not find it in me to consider even a hundred pounds as deserving of the term 'only.' Has the man been apprehended?"

He shook his head. "I found out about the situation only moments ago. I will see to the details of his apprehension in the morning."

She snorted derisively. "You will remove your inactive rump from the softness of that chair and call for a carriage. You will then hie yourself to the authorities and see to this matter tonight. Put yourself in motion, you sapskull." She sighed in disgust. "Why must all my sons and grandsons be such asses?" Turning, she stomped from the room and made her way back up the stairs to her quarters.

Behind her Brinsley got to his feet, his hands shaking under the onslaught he had just weathered. "Though she is correct," he muttered, "I would as leave forgo the business as receive the lashing of her tongue in such an instance." Getting his cloak, he left the house and took himself to the city.

Upon leaving the Brinsley House, Currante returned to his rooms, lighted a candle, and quickly exchanged his clothing for a dark suit of shabby appearance. Donning a long cloak, he searched through his wardrobe until he discovered a wide-brimmed, feature-concealing hat. Stepping to a mirror, he placed the hat on his head, tugged once at the brim to bring it down over his upper face. He smiled at the result. "Excellent," he said aloud. Then he opened a drawer and withdrew a pistol.

Moments later, the firearm concealed under the cloak, he left the building and set off at a fast pace toward a slightly better section of the city. Forty minutes after leaving his own flat, he raised a fist to rap at the door of another.

"Who is it?" came the call from within.

"Allow me in, Wright," Currante called. "It has been discovered that you are deserving severance for the time spent with us."

Sounds of movement were definable momentarily, then the door swung open and a small pale-faced man peered out. "Currante," he said, "what is it you say of severance? Brinsley has never considered such a thing to my knowledge."

Stepping into the room past the bookkeeper, Currante chuckled. "Even he realizes when he has been in error, my friend. Though it is not in him to admit such a thing, he is sorry to have terminated you. He chooses to send a paltry sum to soothe his conscience."

Swinging the door shut, Wright said, "Oh, that I were in a position to advise him as to what he could do with his conscience payment. But I must eat until another position can be found. How much am I to receive?"

"A pittance," Currante answered, his glance swinging around the apartment. "Would you have a drink of anything for a messenger who brings you funds?"

"Of course. My manners are lacking," Wright answered, stepping past the taller man. "There is still a tot of rum about, I believe." He bent to a cabinet and began searching through it.

Swiftly Currante moved to position behind the man and withdrew the pistol. The next moment flint fell and a ball entered the head of the former bookkeeper. "Rest well, Wright," Currante said, lifting the man to move him to a chair. He placed the pistol in the dead hand and released his grip. The lifeless hand fell to the side of the corpse, and the gun dropped to the floor.

With a final glance around the room Currante made his way to the door, opened it a crack, and, seeing no one, stepped swiftly to the hallway and left the building. He was humming a tune when an' hour later, again dressed for business, he stepped from his apartment and headed for the offices of Brinsley Enterprises.

CHAPTER TEN

Melissa awoke before the sun kissed the morning. Instantly her thoughts turned to the amazing events of the previous night, and she hugged her pillow in happiness. "I cannot believe it," she said aloud. "I cannot believe such a thing has happened to me." She rose from bed, glanced at the porcelain clock on the nightstand, and hurried from the room in hopes of speaking with her great-grandmother before others were about.

"Come in, Missy," the duchess called at the soft tap on her bedroom door.

Opening the door, Melissa fixed the loved one with an impish glance and asked, "And how were you to know it was I, Grandmother?"

The duchess chuckled. "Why, child, when one of your age settles herself for the night with her first love to fill her thoughts, there is little doubt but that she will awaken early and search out the answers to questions that have presented themselves during the dreaming period. I awakened an hour ago but chose to remain here until you arrived." She patted the edge of the bed. "Sit here and ease yourself of the questions that drive you."

Moving to sit on the bed, Melissa asked, "You

know everything concerning anyone and anything, do you not, Grandmother?"

"Hardly." The older woman laughed. "I do, however, attempt to know those I become acquainted with. Now, tell me, are your sympathies as they were last night?"

"Oh, yes, yes, yes," the girl answered, smiling. "I cannot believe that such a thing has happened to Melissa Brinsley. Oh, Grandmother, tell me. Was it like this when you and the duke first met?"

The old eyes clouded slightly in memory. "It was, child. It was, in fact, much the same as you have experienced. The duke was known as a rake through all of Europe. It was not in my father to allow such a person to lay claim to his only daughter." She nodded her head as if nearly asleep. "Yes, I know what you are feeling. May the good Lord see that your future is as pleasant and rewarding as mine was."

Melissa dropped her glance, saying, "Am I foolish to hope that he will find me enough to his liking to want me for a wife, Grandmother?"

"Look at me, child," the duchess ordered. When Melissa had done so, she continued, "Any who lives without hope for love shared is indeed a fool. Where Mr. Boyden is concerned, I sense you have little concern. He is smitten with you."

The instant smile on the girl's face mirrored the relief she felt. "Oh, please, tell me of your conversation with him after I left. Please, Grandmother."

"I will only tell you that he feels he has found that which every man dreams of in the way of true love. Now, if you can control the expression of complete ecstacy you wear, we should take ourselves downstairs and greet your parents." She chuckled, adding, "If they were to see you this moment, they would wonder at your sanity. Get to your feet and go. I shall follow in minutes."

"Yes, Grandmother," Melissa answered, standing. "Oh, has any heart felt as mine does this instant?"

"Never, I'm sure," the old woman answered. "Leave the room. I would get from this bed in privacy."

Turning happily, the girl left and made her way down the stairs to the dining room. The happiness left her face when she encountered her father's morose expression. Crossing to take her place at the breakfast table, she first sent a glance at her mother, then asked, "And, Father, what has you so deep in the doldrums this lovely morning?"

His glance came up to her and he sat for a moment as if unaware of her presence. Then, with a shake of his head, he said, "It is nothing for you to concern yourself with, Melissa. It is only a business matter. Was there sign of your grandmother as you left your room?"

"She will be with us presently," the girl answered, turning to her mother. "And, Mother, is it also business that has taken your smile?"

"Nonsense," her mother snapped. "There is little I would know of any business problems. It was only the unsettling of all I ate last night that kept me awake. The presence of that—that Colonist and his easy manner with the duchess did much against my digestion."

"I thought him to be quite unique," Melissa answered as a servant placed breakfast before her.

"And who are we discussing now?" the duchess asked, entering the room.

"Mr. Boyden, Grandmother," the girl answered. "Mother claims his presence turned her stomach."

"Hummph," the old woman snorted as she settled to her place at the table. Then her glance swung to Brinsley. "And, Reginald, what of your errand last night?"

He faced her guiltily. "The authorities assured me they would begin investigating the moment I took my leave, Grandmother. They promised me a report at the earliest. There is nothing to be concerned with, I'm certain."

"If that is the look of one who is certain of such a thing, I would detest seeing the look of a worried person," she retorted. "Is it known if the bookkeeper has taken himself from the city since leaving your employment?"

He shook his head. "It is not known. They assured me they would call on his former place of residence before morning and attempt to learn of his whereabouts from the owner of the building.

110

They are very efficient, Grandmother. Do not allow this to alter your mood."

She attacked the breakfast set before her and, in the midst of chewing, informed him, "The alteration of my mood was done some days ago when your father required some forty thousand pounds on the instant. Should such a thing happen in this occurrence, there would be little I could do to assist you at the time. The duchy is, at present, lacking in extraneous funds."

He sighed heavily. "Grandmother, there is nothing to concern yourself about. The few hundred pounds, if indeed it turns out to be even that, will not put me in a position to require your assistance. All who extend credit to me know that they are safe. An extension on any or all of the due statements will be of no consequence."

"I certainly hope you are correct. I—" She broke off as the butler entered the room.

"Yes, what is it?" Brinsley asked, relieved at the interruption.

"A gentleman to see you. He has the identification of the crown and says he has information you wish."

"Aha!" Brinsley said, wiping his mouth with a napkin. "They've caught the beggar." He stood as if to leave the table.

"Have the gentleman shown in," the duchess ordered. "Allow all of us to receive the good news with you."

Reluctantly, Brinsley, nodded to the butler. When the servant had gone, he said, "I doubt the man will feel comfortable interrupting our meal, Grandmother."

She was saved an answer by the entrance of a broad-shouldered, heavily paunched man. With a glance at all present he announced, "Sir Reginald, ladies, forgive me for calling at such a moment. We did, however, promise Sir Reginald information at the earliest time possible."

"Yes. Yes, man," Brinsley said. "What information do you have for me? Did you locate Wright?"

"We did that, sir. He was in his rooms."

"And the money he'd stolen?"

The officer shook his head. "There was no sign of any money or any record within his quarters, sir."

"But he can be made to tell the whereabouts of it, can he not?" Brinsley asked, a hint of uncertainty in his voice.

Again the paunchy one shook his head. "Afraid that is past the possible, sir. If the ladies will pardon me, the rest of the report is not the thing to go with a meal."

"Nonsense," the duchess snapped. "Finish what you have to say, man. We are all concerned with this situation."

"Very well, madam," he nodded. "It seems Mr. Wright took his own life shortly before we arrived at his rooms, sir. Put a ball in his head, he did.

112

Did a right smart job of snuffing himself. There's nothing will be learned from the lips of that one."

"Dead?" Brinsley exclaimed. "Impossible! He couldn't . . . The money he stole . . . I—"

"Sit down before you have an attack, Reginald," the duchess ordered, her glance going to the officer. "You say there was no record or any other indication of the whereabouts of his money?"

"No, madam. He had only a pound or two in his keeping. The landlord says the man was behind in his rent and bills. It seems odd he would be in such straits, having taken the amount reported by Sir Reginald." He shrugged and added, "But he is not the first to become a thief because of gambling debts or other promises to pay. Well, Sir Reginald, that—for the present—is the sum of it. I must return. We will, of course, keep you posted on anything we discover." With a nod to all he turned to leave.

"Thank you, sir," the duchess called after him. Then she turned to Brinsley. "Well, Reginald, it would seem your worry is not misplaced. I am glad the amount is no more than it is. At the moment I would be sorely put to assist you."

Brinsley appeared to be in a state of shock. For a long moment he sat staring at the empty doorway through which the officer had left, then in a mumble he said, "Pray there is no more than Ashley thought."

"Ashley, Father?" Melissa asked. "Is it Ashley

Currante and this Wright fellow who are at the bottom of your troubles?"

"What?" he asked, snapping himself back to the moment. "Ashley? No, of course not. It was Ashley's quick eye that caught the errors in the books. Had it not been for him, the theft would have gone unnoticed until such time as the shortage could have proven embarrassing."

"You are fortunate to have one of such acumen with you, Reginald," Lady Brinsley said. "Now finish eating. You must have your strength if you are to go to the office today."

"I have eaten all I care for," he told her, getting to his feet. "I must hie myself to the city and speak with Ashley to determine the true amount of the theft. I shall return at the earliest." He left the room, barely acknowledging the presence of his daughter and his grandmother.

An expression of worry on her face, Melissa said, "Father seems most upset over this event, Mother. Is there anything to be done to ease his concern?"

Lady Brinsley shook her head in a negative answer. "There is nothing any of us can do, Melissa. Your father seldom discusses business with me. Until moments ago, I was not aware of his reason for leaving last night."

"Proving once again that he is a fool," the duchess said, resuming her eating.

"That is unfair, Grandmother," Melissa said.

"Father is eaten with worry at this moment. I sympathize with him."

"As do I," the old lady said. "However, like his father and uncles, any sympathies shown him tend to relax him in the performance of his duties. Though the few hundred pounds is not a great amount, it will be difficult at this moment for me to acquire the sum." She smiled softly then and sent her glance to Lady Brinsley. "Edith, do not fear. Your husband, though irritated at me constantly, realizes that he must be pushed at times. He further realizes that if within my power, I will not see him come to ruin."

Lady Brinsley's head came up and her mouth dropped open. "But . . . I believed . . . you have said so many times that—"

"Nonsense. He is a Brinsley. I will allow no Brinsley or their people to suffer at the end mark. If the few hundred pounds cannot be recovered, I shall speak with a friend and replace it."

Relief was evident in the audible sigh that escaped Lady Brinsley's lips. "Ah, Grandmother, your words are as rays of sunlight on a clouded day. I—"

"Enough," the old woman said. "Your breakfast grows cold." Her glance shifted to Melissa, who sat smiling across the table at her. "And what has touched you as humorous, girl?" she demanded.

With a chuckle of satisfaction Melissa shook her head. "Nothing, Grandmother. It only strikes me

115

as odd that few know you as I do. Thank you for all of us."

"Bah!" was the retort as the old woman continued eating.

Upon arriving at the business site, Brinsley immediately searched out Currante. He found the representative, with his head on his arms, sound asleep at the bookkeeper's desk. Gripping the sleeper's shoulder, he shook him awake. "Ashley, my man, wake up. For God's sake, I did not intend that you spend the entire night at the books. Wake up, man."

Groggily, Currante shook his head. Then, yawning widely, he said, "It was necessary that the time be spent, sir. Though the news is not good, I have compiled a total of that which was taken from the business."

"Yes? And what was the total? Quickly, man. Tell me."

Currante yawned again, asked pardon, and said, "I fear our Mr. Wright has some sixty thousand pounds to repay when he is apprehended, sir. The sum came to sixty-two thousand to be exact."

Brinsley paled at the words. "Sixty-two thousand pounds?" he got out in a strangled tone. "It cannot be, Ashley. It is impossible. It—"

"It is true, sir," Currante assured him. "However there is little cause of concern. The authorities will see that Wright comes up with his stolen gains once they apprehend him."

Brinsley shook his head as if stricken dumb. "The man is dead. Killed himself last night. There is no indication of the whereabouts of the money. Oh, my God, I am ruined. The Brinsley Enterprises are no more. I—" Having gotten up from his chair, Currante crossed to his employer and placed an arm around the sagging shoulders. "Surely, sir, your father—"

"—is in severe straits himself," Brinsley nearly sobbed. "I only this morning found out. Oh, my God."

"The duchess, sir. Though I profess to have little liking for her, surely she will—"

Brinsley shook his head. "She cannot at this time. My father required a goodly sum. It has placed the duchess in an unhelpful position." His head came up, and the stricken expression deepened. "Good Lord, I must now go inform her of the true state of things." He turned from under the consoling arm of Currante and headed for the door.

The beginnings of a sardonic smile twisted the lips of the representative as his employer stepped across the room. Suddenly, as Brinsley reached for the door, the smile again became an expression of sympathy. "Sir," he called, "though I would not wish to intrude on your business, if all else fails, I

117

have a friend who might lend me funds to assist you in your plight."

Turning back to face the man, Brinsley sighed. "Ah, Ashley, that every man could have one such as you in his employ. No, man, I would not ask that of you. I shall face my grandmother with the news, and we shall, after her tirade is completed, find a way, hopefully."

Currante nodded. "Very well, sir. However, if necessary . . ."

"My thanks, Ashley. You are a gentleman of the first rank. Now I must take myself to Brinsley House and speak with the duchess." Turning, he left the room.

He was unaware of the soft laughter that followed him as he stepped from the business and entered the carriage to return home.

CHAPTER ELEVEN

Brinsley wore the expression of a whipped dog when he left the carriage to enter Brinsley House. Relinquishing his cape and hat to the butler, he asked that the duchess be informed of his return. "Ask that she allow me a moment of her time in the library also," he added as the butler made to leave.

Moments later the duchess entered the library and crossed to look down at him as he sat behind the desk. "I was told you wished to speak to me, Reginald," she said, her green eyes evaluating his expression. "What seems to be the problem?"

"I cannot find the words to explain it, Grandmother. I can only say Grandfather was a fool to entrust me with such responsiblity as he did."

"Your grandfather was far from a fool," she said, her tone softening. "Now tell me. What has brought you to your present state?"

Brinsley swallowed heavily and met the old eyes. "The business and all I own is gone, Grandmother." Grief as well as defeat were alive in his voice. "There is nothing left. And there is nothing to be done about the situation."

"Nonsense," she answered. "There is always

something that can be done. What was the total amount removed from the business?"

"Sixty-two thousand pounds, Grandmama. Though Ashley did not say it, I am aware that many due payments have been ignored, certainly concealed, in the far past. There is no other way the amount could have come to such staggering figures."

"Sixty-two thousand pounds?" she echoed. "By all that's holy, Reginald, the amount in itself is a fortune."

He nodded sadly. "And I've borrowed heavily on the property. Had this not come about the profits from investments would have been . . ." He ceased speaking to drop his head to his hands as if crying.

The old woman looked down at her grandson for several long silent moments. Suddenly her lips thinned into a line and the eyes narrowed. "Have you no friends to turn to, Reginald?"

The shrug of his shoulders was indicative of his temperament. "None of such stature that they would consider such a loan, even if they were able to lend that amount. I fear I am not of the winning personality Grandfather was." Suddenly the hands dropped and his head came up. "I am in error, Grandmother. There is one who until this day I did not consider a close friend. Ashley made mention that he might indeed assist me if all else fails." A ray of hope entered his eyes at the words.

"Currante?" she asked. "Currante has offered to lend you such a large amount?"

"Not him, Grandmother. A friend of his. It is a method. My shock at hearing the state of my affairs had so unsettled me that till this moment the words he spoke escaped me." He relaxed visibly. "Perhaps the moment is not as black as I had supposed."

The duchess eyed him thoughtfully. "Did Mr. Currante speak the name of this friend?"

"No, Grandmother, but Ashley would not say a thing unless it was true. What difference who the friend is? All that will be required is a loan until such time as the money can be recovered."

"The authorities have said there is no indication of the whereabouts of the money," she reminded him. "What makes you believe there will be a recovery?"

"Ah, Grandmother," he said, his mood lightening, "the authorities are very efficient. I have no doubt that they will discover it soon. Until that time I shall speak with Ashley of his friend."

"The offer made by Mr. Currante is truly a generous one, Reginald, but let us first consider if the thing can be handled within the circle of the family. I will require my carriage. I must go to the city."

He sobered slightly and nodded. "Of course, Grandmother. However there is little cause for concern at this point. With the loan from Ashley's friend, Brinsley Enterprises will survive until such time as the authorities accomplish an end to their investigation and return the stolen money to me."

"Has mention been made of the charge for this loan?"

The animation left his face for a moment, then, a tight smile on his lips, he said, "There has been no discussion of the loan at all as yet. However I have no fear of Ashley allowing his friend to overcharge me."

She was silent for another long moment before nodding. "Well, let us first see if it is possible to handle the situation in another way. See to my carriage. And I would appreciate the company of Missy, if she is not needed here."

"Of course, Grandmother. Do not concern yourself overmuch." Getting to his feet, he followed the old woman from the room and left the house to see to the carriage.

The duchess waited until her grandson had gone before making her way to the parlor to speak with Lady Brinsley and Melissa. They were both present when she entered.

Melissa looked up at the old woman. "Ah, Grandmother, the servants have said you were closeted with Father. What is the news?"

"Bad, I fear. I must take myself to the city as soon as possible. The carriage is being readied at this moment." Her glance swung to Lady Brinsley.

"I would have the company of Melissa, if I may, Edith."

Lady Brinsley's eyes widened in surprise that it had been a request rather than an order. She nodded, "Certainly, Grandmother. Will you be gone long?"

"There is no way of knowing." She hesitated, then to both of them said, "You are both members of the family. Therefore you have a right to know what passes. The total of the missing funds is sixty-two thousand pounds. For all intents and purposes Reginald is ruined to the last foot of property and the last stitch of clothing. It is for this reason I go to the city today."

Both women inhaled sharply at the disclosure. Finally Melissa asked, "Is it possible to replace such a huge amount, Grandmother?"

The old woman nodded. "Reginald has a method, though I do not care for it. I hope this situation will not leave the circle of our family and close friends. Come, child, let us go to the city. There is much that needs to be seen to."

Some thirty minutes later, as the carriage carried them swiftly along the streets of the city, the duchess called to the driver to stop. When he stepped from the seat to attend her, she said, "The Red Boar Inn will be our first destination. Make haste, for the hour grows late." She settled back against the cushion and fixed her great-granddaughter with a studious glance. "Tell me, Missy," she said, finally breaking into the silence that had held the girl for a major portion of the trip, "can you consider Brett Boyden in an objective manner?"

"Brett?" the girl asked in surprise. "I—I don't know what you mean, Grandmother."

"Has love for him blinded you to all else about him or can you look at him and make an honest appraisal of his talents?"

"I fear I would of necessity claim that he must be the finest in anything, Grandmother. What is it you speak of?"

"Does he strike you as one who would remain calm and logical in a situation of stress, girl?"

Melissa chuckled lightly. "And laugh in the face of such a situation, if I judge him right. I fear my words and impressions mean little though. One might well say I am prejudiced where Brett is concerned."

The duchess nodded. "And rightly so, unless I misguess. Well, we shall see."

"Do you intend to speak with Brett of this situation, Grandmother?"

"I do. Does that bother you?"

Melissa hesitated a second. "It seems unusual that you would allow such a confidence with him, considering the length of time he has been acquainted with us."

The old eyes sparkled and a half smile threatened the old woman's lips. "I feel I have known Brett for as many years as I have known Charlie. There is that about the man that rejects any manner of false behavior."

Melissa was alive with pleasure at the words. "Oh, Grandmother, I wish I could in some way express my feelings to you for what you have brought about. It is beyond gratitude. It is—"

"—a portion of a grandmother's duties," the duchess finished for her. "Now, we near the inn. See to your bonnet. It has taken itself to a point from center."

Melissa was straightening the bonnet when the carriage slowed and drew to a stop in front of the Red Boar Inn. She sent a glance toward the shop and turned a questioning look at the older woman. "What is here, Grandmother? Are you hungry?"

"Cease your questioning, girl. You shall know soon enough. Come."

They removed themselves from the carriage, crossed the walk, and entered the establishment. Instantly the innkeeper was before them, asking, "And what is it I can do to serve the duchess this day?"

The duchess looked down at him. "The gentleman I spoke with yesterday, is he stationed in his usual place?"

"He is, your Grace. Shall I announce you?"

She stepped past him with Melissa following. "That will not be necessary. I would partake of a draft of your famous ale. The girl will have tea."

"At once, your Grace," he said to her back as she stepped purposely toward the curtained booth.

Arriving at the booth, the old woman pulled the curtain back and looked at Brett Boyden. "I fear I'm becoming a pest to you at your lunch moment, Brett, but there is a matter on which I would like your advice."

There was obvious pleasure in his expression when he said, "My time is yours for any purpose, Carrie. For what you have done in my service, there can never be sufficient payment." Then his eyes fell on the girl standing behind her great-grandmother. His smile broadened, and the gray eyes took on a totally different light. "Ah, Missy," he said, "your grandmother must be the finest of angels. Come sit with me. We shall dine together."

The innkeeper came upon the scene at that moment, bearing ale and tea. When these had been placed on the table, he took leave, and the duchess seated herself across from Boyden. Melissa stood for a moment as if undecided.

"Well, child," the duchess asked, humorously, "are you to follow the demands of society or the craving of your heart?"

"I . . ." Melissa began, color flowing into her cheeks. "Grandmother, I am not aware of your meaning. I—"

"You wonder at the effect if you should choose to take a seat next to Brett, rather than beside your grandmother. Well, child, use your eyes. The curtain conceals all that takes place within this area. Pull it and put your heart at ease."

Smiling in spite of her embarrassment, Melissa stepped into the booth and drew the curtain shut. Then, taking a seat beside Boyden, she faced him. "I fear I am shameless, Brett," she said. "I confess I wish to be as close as possible to you."

"And I to you," he answered, his head tilted back a bit that he might meet her eyes. "You are more than lovely this day, Missy."

"Enough," the duchess said. "I shall drink my ale. In the course of that drink I will not be able to notice if the two of you should do something improper, such as kissing one another. I assume you will remember your places." So saying, she lifted the tankard to her lips and closed her eyes.

Chuckling, Brett reached to pull the girl's head down slightly. Their lips met and held for a long moment's embrace. The sound of the tankard striking the table moments later brought an end to the kiss. They gave their attention to the duchess.

Ignoring the pleased, dreamy expression on her great-granddaughter's face, she met Boyden's glance squarely. "I am in need of your intelligence and business acumen, Brett. Are you occupied for the next several hours?"

His disarming smile flashed at the question. "Never will there be such an occupation of my time that would allow me to refuse a request of yours, Carrie. What can I do to aid you?"

Lifting the tankard of ale, she said, "Finish your drink. If we are to lunch together, as I would wish it, we must make haste to another place. The person I mentioned I wished you to meet at a later date is imperative to our conversation and decision. We shall go to his residence." She tipped the tankard and took a long draft.

Without question Brett followed her action. When he had drained the tankard, he wiped his lips. "I assume this friend is aware of the tribe that shall in a short time invade his privacy," he said.

The duchess shook her head. "It will make no matter. Charlie will welcome us, I'm certain." Her glance swung to Melissa. "Remove your head from the clouds, child. Finish your drink. There is much to be done and you detain Brett and me in the doing." There was no sting of admonishment in the words. Again tipping the tankard, she drained it.

Melissa snapped herself back to the moment and, blushing heavily, drank her tea. Then by common consent they removed themselves from the booth and made their way outside to the carriage. When the driver had been given directions and they were all seated comfortably, Melissa said, "Grandmother, would that every girl had such a one as you to forward her life as you do mine."

The old lady nodded, her glance taking in both young people. "I would see nothing wasted if it were within my powers to prevent it. Today's meeting with Brett was a certainty. I saw no reason that it should not serve the purpose of you as well as myself, Missy. However when we arrive at the earl's home, you must restrain your emotions and put your mind to what is said. There may eventually come a time when you will be called upon to use your thoughts to a purpose resembling the one we face. Do you understand my meaning, both of you?"

Boyden studied her momentarily before saying, "I feel there is something afoot that affects you deeply, Carrie. If it is anything I can see to, consider it taken care of."

"My thanks, Brett. We shall shortly see what is to be done. Now I would nap. See that the two of you contain yourselves until we reach the earl's house." So saying, she turned her head to the side and leaned back against the cushion, her eyes closed as if in sleep.

"Ah, Carrie," Brett chuckled, raising himself to bend over the old woman and place his lips against her cheek. "There is, on my part at least, no need for you to feign sleep that Missy and I might enjoy the closeness we share. I would have you see my next action and know that I love your granddaughter."

The duchess brought her head back to normal and opened her eyes. "Have you no sense of decency?" she asked as he pulled the girl to him and kissed her soundly.

When their lips had separated, he turned to the duchess, matching her smile. "None whatever where Missy is concerned. Have you told her of my words following our last meeting?"

"That, I believe, is for you to do, Brett," the old woman answered. "Be certain of your feelings before speaking though. Remember my words to you in the garden."

He nodded and turned to Melissa who sat waiting, her eyes steady on the man she loved. "I have informed your grandmother—Carrie—that I wish to take you as my wife. Though I can only guess at your feelings toward me, I hope my brashness does not aggravate your senses."

She inhaled sharply, paled slightly, then sighed. "Oh. Oh, Brett. I cannot. There is not the time for me to—"

"—indulge in more than one final kiss before we arrive at the earl's," the duchess finished for her. "Let your touch speak for you, child." She chuckled lightly as she completed the statement, for neither of them were paying the least bit of attention to her.

As the embrace ended, the carriage drew to a

stop at the earl's door. The butler, who had earlier hesitated at announcing the duchess, greeted them and led them without hesitation into the house.

"Carrie!" the earl exclaimed in pleasure as they entered the study. "My fortunes are improving to have the opportunity to see you twice in as many days." Taking her hands in his, he kissed her cheeks, then shifted his attention to the two young ones. "And who is with you?"

"The starry-eyed lass is the daughter of my grandson, Reginald Brinsley. The equally starry-eyed lad is Brett Boyden of the United States. Children, the Earl of Morgan."

The earl moved to accept Melissa's hand and bend over it. Straightening, he studied her features and smiled. "You are nearly as lovely as Carrie, child. Ah, it is as if I've stepped into the beloved past and am again looking into the eyes of the most beautiful woman in all Europe."

Melissa nodded, a smile on her face. "I am complimented, sir. To be so compared with my grandmother is the highest tribute anyone could pay me. She is as beautiful as you say."

"And stubborn to the nth degree," he told her. "She continues to refuse my offers of marriage no matter how I phrase them." He turned to Boyden, offering a hand. "Sir, welcome to my house. If you are a friend of Carrie's, then you are, by the same token, a friend of mine. Welcome."

Accepting the hand, Brett nodded. "Carrie, were she but younger, would not be yours without a battle, sir, for she is, indeed, the toast of any and all who meet her."

The earl's eyes narrowed at his use of the duchess's first name. Turning, he faced the older woman. "From your expression, Carrie, I see he really is a close friend. This is the gentleman you asked of yesterday, is it not?"

"It is, Charlie," she answered.

He turned back to Boyden. "Then, sir, consider yourself of a rank equal to kings. For there are those of royalty who dare not refer to my beloved Carrie in so personal a manner."

"And now," the duchess broke in, "if this senile fool has wasted himself to the limit with compliments to turn my head, could we possibly get to the matter at hand?"

The earl shrugged. "Ah, well, children, she will ever put me off in my devotions. Very well, what is it, Carrie?"

"First, Charlie, I fear we must impose ourselves upon you for lunch. We have not eaten. Then we must have your excellent thoughts on a problem of some importance."

He nodded in satisfaction. "The problem you shall relate to me over the lunch, Carrie. My thoughts would be yours when I know what it is that bothers you." He turned, leading them into the dining room.

* * *

Some thirty minutes later, when luncheon had been served and consumed, the duchess said, "And that, Charlie, is the tale. What I wish from you is direction in what is to be done."

The earl stroked his chin in thought for a moment. "It will require conversion of some holdings and the estate at Brighton, but I see no great reason for concern, Carrie."

She shook her head and smiled knowingly at him. "Ah, Charlie, how like you. I would not and could not ask you to relinquish your remaining fortunes for such a problem as this. I wish you to think of another solution."

"Your pardon, Carrie," Brett interrupted, breaking the silence both he and Melissa had held since the moment the duchess had begun relating the story to the earl. "Though I am not certain as to what this sixty-two thousand pounds would amount to in American money, I assure you that in but a month—two at the most—I could gather the sum together and return with it."

Again she shook her head. "You, Brett, fast become the equal of Charlie in my estimation. There is little wonder Missy is so taken with you. But, as with Charlie, I cannot and will not allow such a thing. No, the money that is missing is surely some place to be found. It requires only that we locate it and return it to its rightful place."

"And if we cannot?" the earl asked.

She sighed and looked at her plate. "Then, Charlie, I shall convert the total of my properties, if necessary, to accumulate the needed sum."

"And then?" he asked.

She chuckled. "And then, friend Charlie, I shall be forced to hold you to your words of endearment. I shall call upon you to honor the romantic proposals you have made in my direction for the past forty years."

He met her smile with a serious expression. "Then may we never locate the blasted money." He hesitated a moment before relaxing and allowing a smile to take him. "You do not make it easy for me to think of ways to assist you in finding the money, Carrie. Had I known all these years that a situation such as this would present me with the opportunity to have you as my own, I should have endeavored to remove the total amount of your grandson's fortune myself." Sending a glance at the smiling young people, he said, "Let us return to the study if everyone has completed the meal." So saying, he stood and offered the duchess his hand, his manner once again thoughtful.

CHAPTER TWELVE

Shortly after the duchess and Melissa had left the property, Reginald Brinsley made his way to the parlor and faced his wife. "Edith," he said, "though the moment is one of tribulation, there is no cause for you to be concerned. It is nothing that cannot be seen to."

Meeting his glance, she straightened. "Reginald, since our first meeting I have never taken undue interest in or pressed you for information concerning the business. Grandmother, though unduly harsh in her estimation, has stated that you are a fool for not allowing me to be a portion of what you do. I believe that both of us are fools. We are man and wife, therefore, what affects one affects the other. I believe sixty-two thousand pounds to be of a serious nature. Am I wrong?"

For a long moment he stared at her in disbelief. Then, with a shake of his head, he said. "Your manner takes me by surprise, Edith. I judge from your words that Grandmama has informed you of the total problem facing Brinsley Enterprises." She nodded and he continued. "Very well, then, perhaps she and you are correct. Perhaps I have taken too much for granted in assuming that you had no interest in the humdrum happenings of the business world."

"I have an interest in anything that is part of you, Reginald," she told him. "Is there truly a method known to you whereby we might salvage the business?"

He nodded. "Indeed, there is. Ashley Currante has offered to lend me the necessary money to continue until such time as the authorities discover the whereabouts of the funds taken by Wright. I was surprised by his offer. My estimation of him, though high to begin with, has escalated this day."

A puzzled expression took her features. "Ashley? Beg pardon, Reginald, but where could Ashley possibly have amassed such a fortune as is needed?"

He chuckled humorously at the question. "Ah, Edith—you and Grandmama. The fortune is not Ashley's but belongs to a friend of his. Ashley has offered to speak in my behalf and engineer a loan through a friend of his. So, you see, there is no real cause for concern. I shall take the loan until such time as my money is returned. Then, with a new bookkeeper—one who shall be watched constantly—Brinsley Enterprises will continue as before."

He turned toward the door, adding, "Grandmama wishes to consider other sources first, so I must return to the business and advise Ashley that there is no certainty that his aid will be necessary. I shall dine in the city and will return home as soon as possible." With that he donned his cloak and hat and left the house.

Behind him Edith Brinsley sat in thoughtful silence for several minutes before shaking her head and muttering, "Ah, to have the wisdom of the duchess on such occasions."

Ashley Currante was busying himself around the Brinsley offices when his employer entered with a smile of good cheer on his face. Advancing to take Brinsley's cloak and hat, he said, "And, sir, do I take it you have come upon unknown funds to replenish Brinsley Enterprises?"

Brinsley chuckled. "Ah, Ashley, in truth it was your offer of assistance that, when realization dawned on me, altered my mood. There is no question that the authorities will return the purloined money to me soon. Until that time I need only borrow the use of funds to remain solvent."

Currante wore a barely controlled smile at the words. "Do you then wish me to speak with my friend of the amount, sir?"

Brinsley shook his head. "No, man—though I do appreciate the offer. The duchess is at this moment within the city in search of a method to handle the problem within the circle of the family. Though irritating at times, she has ever come up with solutions to all the family problems. It will only be under the direst circumstances that I shall ask you to place yourself in such a position to me."

The black eyes narrowed momentarily, then the representative said, "Of course, Sir Brinsley. Though it would serve me with pleasure to be able to assist you at this time, I agree with the duchess. Such things should be kept within family bounds, if at all possible." He paused thoughtfully. "Would it be possible for me to leave early today, sir? There are matters of a personal nature that I must see to."

"Of course, man." Brinsley laughed expansively. "Go whenever you wish. And see that you gain some rest. Your time spent here during the past night will more than serve to replace any time you are absent. I shall handle what is necessary this day and see that the building is locked."

"Thank you, sir," Currante said with a nod. "I have but another hour's work to see to here, then I shall leave."

"Gem of a man," Brinsley murmured to himself as the representative stepped to another section of the office.

CHAPTER THIRTEEN

When Melissa and Boyden had seated themselves in the study, the earl turned to the duchess. "Is this Ashley Currante the same one you wished information on earlier?" he asked.

"The same, Charles. The man is odious, to say the least. His manner leaves me cold as to the methods of human nature. There is something about him that resembles a snake."

"Beg pardon," Boyden put in. "Is it possible I know this Currante?"

Melissa smiled at him. "Not formally, Brett. However, he did inform me that you had approached him on the day of the demonstration and asked about me." In a few words she gave a description of the man in question.

"It strikes me as odd that such a person would have so great an amount of money at his calling. The question is why he labors in the position of hired lackey when such an available fortune could assure him of success in business of his own."

"Excellent reasoning, Boyden," the earl said approvingly. He turned to the duchess. "Carrie, what are your thoughts on the matter? Obviously you are not in favor of your grandson accepting this man's help. Is there a reason other than the fact that you dislike Currante?"

She sat for a moment, the old eyes narrowed in thought. Then, her head coming up, she said, "I sense he is a portion of the reason for my having the dream, Charlie. What of your investigation of him?"

"Much too early to know anything of importance, Carrie. You did say you wished to know all there is to know of him. That, I fear, takes time. At this point I fear I can only tell you his address. A good man is taking note of his every move however, so within the next few days he might very well be aware of the man as a whole."

The duchess nodded. "Of course. I expect too much too soon. You said you have his address. Is he living beyond that which he supposedly earns?"

"Hardly," the earl answered, giving the address. "His apartment, if indeed it can be called such a thing, is in one of the lowest sections of the city. Though entry has not been made into his particular section of the building, the others available are barely more than trash heaps. No, if lodging is any indication, he is as poor as the proverbial church mouse."

"Odd," the duchess said to no one in particular. Then, turning to Melissa, she asked, "Does your father pay the man as well as it would seem?"

The girl nodded. "Quite well, I'm certain, Grandmother. I find it difficult to believe he lives in the squalor indicated by the earl."

"Very strange," the old woman repeated. "I would give much to know what passes through the man's mind. Well, we've taken enough of your time, Charlie. Should you learn anything that could aid our situation, I would appreciate hearing of it."

"Carrie, Carrie," he said, crossing to take her hands in his, "allow me to liquidate a few unessential holdings and solve your grandson's problems. There is little sense in retaining such things at my age. I would deem it an honor."

"Nonsense. If that were the solution I wished, I would—as stated—do the same myself. No, there must be a way. I shall think on it." She turned to the young ones. "Come, Missy, we must return to Brinsley House," she said. "And you, Brett. I believe you should dine with the family again tomorrow evening. I will inform my grandson of it. I shall also see that an invitation is extended to this Currante person. It would, I believe, serve well for you to observe him." So saying, she turned back to the earl, thanked him, and led the way from the house.

Several minutes later she and Melissa parted company with Boyden at the Red Boar Inn and proceeded toward Brinsley House.

* * *

For most of the trip Melissa remained silent, her eyes steady on her great-grandmother. Finally, when the old woman seemed to be so deep in thought that nothing could penetrate her shell, the girl asked, "Grandmother, are your thoughts entirely on Ashley Currante?"

The old head snapped up, the eyes sharp and alert. "No, child. Currante is but a small portion of my thoughts. The overall picture evades me, and it gives me a moment's concern."

"Can it be as bad as your manner suggests, Grandmother? I confess, I cannot imagine a state where the Brinsleys would have financial problems of any great bearing."

"Ah, yes, child," the old woman said, "you as all others who are born to wealth know little of the trials that can befall mankind. It is a fault with our society. In truth, though, I would have none other than yourself know of this: The recent wars and the expansion of the crown have all but drained the duchy of its resources. Due to your father's need of funds lately, the duchy is on the edge of bankruptcy. That is the reason I would have Brett study this Currante fellow. I must admit that I could be mistaken about the man. If that is so, then his offer of loan will be welcome. For, in truth, the holdings of the duchy are at this time deep in the hands of creditors."

This disclosure struck new fear into Melissa. At

the same time she felt an overpowering sympathy for the proud old lady who sat across from her in the carriage. "The earl's offer, Grandmother. Is it not possible—"

"No," the woman interrupted. "Though Charlie would have it seem otherwise, his fortune is much the same as my own and all others of our station in England. I will not see him come to ruin because of me or mine."

"But the offer made by Brett. I—"

"There is no time, girl. Though the offer was a valid one and appreciated, by the time he had gone to America, amassed the needed money and returned, Brinsley Enterprises and the duchy would be in ruins. No, another method must be found. If the offer by Mr. Currante is the only method to present itself, then so be it. I must take care to treat the man with the respect due such an offer. It will not be easy, I fear."

Once the carriage bearing the duchess and Melissa had passed from sight, Boyden returned to his booth at the inn and, over ale, contemplated the information he had received that day. During his second ale he came to a decision. Making his way from the inn, he hailed a rental carriage and moments later was on his way toward the residence of Ashley Currante.

He was deep in thought when the driver said, "Here we are, guv'nor. It's the one just across the street there. And—if I may say so, sir—it's hardly the place for a gentleman like yourself."

"What?" Boyden asked, his attention going to the run-down, trashy condition of the area.

"Meaning no disrespect for your wishes, sir," the driver said, "but them that come to this section are usually in search of women of the lowest order. Them as are gentlemen are more often than not foxed and asking for trouble."

Boyden chuckled and thanked the man. Then, stepping from the carriage, he paid his fare and, when the vehicle had gone, stood for a moment or two studying the shoddy building that housed Currante's rooms. He was like that when Currante himself appeared on the scene, moved swiftly to the building entrance, and disappeared inside.

Only moments after the representative's appearance he was followed by a large well-dressed man wearing a bowler hat, who paused momentarily to send a glance into the doorway Currante had taken, and then passed on to take up a watchful position in the next available doorway.

A frown took Boyden's face for a moment, and then relaxed as he recalled the earl's mention of an investigator assigned to Currante. Moving so as to call no attention to himself, he, too, entered a doorway directly across from the lodging house and prepared to wait.

His patience was rewarded some twenty minutes later when Currante stepped from the building, sent a furtive glance around, and turned to walk deeper into the low-class area. Behind him stepped the investigator. After a moment to allow both men to round the corner, Boyden followed.

Some thirty minutes later the pursuit ended. Currante, after sending a cautious look around the area, entered a foul-appearing café that bore a sign reading THE DEVIL'S PIT.

The investigator continued his pace and passed the inn, with only a glance at the doorway, before turning the corner and disappearing from Boyden's sight. Boyden studied the situation for a moment and retraced his steps half a block to a position where he could observe without being seen by anyone stepping from the inn. Checking the time, he settled himself to wait patiently until his quarry should again show himself.

CHAPTER FOURTEEN

Brinsley's carriage came to a stop in the drive at the same moment the duchess and Melissa arrived at Brinsley House. Removing himself from the carriage and noticing theirs, he signaled his driver to pull away. Then he opened the carriage door and offered an assisting hand to his grandmother and daughter.

"Reginald," the duchess asked, "what of the business? Have the authorities made a further report to you?"

"No, Grandmama," he answered. "Did you discover a method of easing the situation?"

"We shall discuss it over tea," she said, making her way into the house.

Sending a glance at his daughter, Brinsley nodded. "Very well, Grandmama. However, whatever the outcome of your day's search, there is little cause for concern. The offer from Ashley is available at any time."

"I'm certain," she answered, entering the house and stepping toward the parlor.

Lady Brinsley stood when they entered the room. On her face was an expression of concerned curiosity. "What news, Reginald?" she asked.

He shook his head. "Nothing more than we knew earlier, Mother. However, Grandmama informed me that we are to discuss her efforts over tea." He stood until the duchess and his daughter had both taken seats. Then, lowering himself to the settee beside his wife, he fixed the older woman with an inquiring glance. "Well, Grandmama, what of your day?"

"First," the duchess began, "I would request that invitations be extended to two persons for dinner tomorrow evening." Her glance was on her grandson as she spoke.

He frowned for a moment before asking, "That Boyden fellow, I suppose?"

She nodded. "He and one other. I would also like your agent, Mr. Currante, to attend the meal with us."

Surprise shone in Brinsley's eyes, then gave way to pleased satisfaction. "You have reconsidered your original opinion of the man, have you?"

"I would speak with him of the loan mentioned. Anyone who makes such a generous offer is due reconsideration, if the offer is a genuine one."

"I assure you, Grandmama, Ashley is a fine man. The offer, had it not been real, would not have been made by him," Brinsley said with confidence.

"Very well, then. Both men shall dine with us. Now, as to the matter of my day's search for funds, I fear there is nothing to be told. The funds in such an amount are not available at this time. I would hasten to point out—before you make further comment of Mr. Boyden's attendance tomorrow night—that he has offered to supply the needed sum to assist you, Reginald. It would seem you are also due to reconsider your thoughts concerning men."

Surprise again shone on Brinsley's face. "Boyden made such an offer? I— For what reason? Why would he, in light of our instant dislike for each other?"

The duchess sent a glance at Melissa and sighed. "Reginald, open your eyes. The dislike you speak of was on your portion alone. Brett found nothing to dislike about you. As to the offer, he made it because he is a good friend of mine. That, for him, is reason enough."

Brinsley hesitated, his hand massaging his chin in thought. "As you say, Grandmama, the offer does cause me to reconsider the man. However, given a choice between him and Ashley, I would rather entrust my finances to Ashley. Why, we—none of us—even know the true business of this Boyden fellow."

"Nor do we of any man alive," the duchess retorted. "That, however, is beside the point. Though the offer was genuine, Brett would find it impossible to return to the United States, raise the amount needed and return in time to salvage the Brinsley fortunes."

Brinsley's mood darkened. "And what of your desire to keep the problem within the family circle? Have you discovered a way?"

She shook her head. "I have not. At this moment such a thing is impossible. Therefore it would seem—if all is as it should be—you may possibly be thankful for Mr. Currante's offer. We shall see."

"Possibly?" Brinsley exhaled. "It would seem there is no choice but to accept his generosity. I, for one, feel not the least qualm about doing such a thing."

"I am glad you are so confident in your employee," the duchess said sincerely. "Now the day grows late. I would dine and take to my bed. There has been much to sap my strength this day."

Together the four rose and made their way to the dining room. Melissa, walking beside her grandmother, asked, "Is it possible Father is seeing Brett in his true light, Grandmother?"

The old woman met her hopeful glance and snorted. "Of course not. He is convinced that to soothe me he must seem to reappraise someone he judged wrongly. At this moment the matter of Brett Boyden has not altered a whit in his judgment. He is consumed with thoughts of the business and his loss, as well he should be."

The girl sighed in sadness. "Ah, that he could but know Brett as you and I know him."

"Given time and the proper circumstances, such will be the case. Now enough of this. Let us dine in peace. Do nothing to irritate your father. I, too, shall be on my best behavior."

"Which alone will shock him beyond belief," Melissa whispered as they entered the dining room. There was a chuckle on both their lips as they took their seats at the table.

Boyden drew a watch from his pocket, saw that he had been waiting more than twenty minutes for Currante to leave the café across the street, and sighed. At the moment of that sigh the representative stepped from the business and, without a glance in either direction, stepped quickly back the way he had come. Moments later, from around the corner, the investigator came into view, following his quarry.

"Fool," Boyden muttered, realizing that Currante had but to turn and lay eyes on the man to know what was afoot. With a shake of his head at the ignorance of the trailer, he set off across the street and entered the café, assuming the staggering walk of one who had more than his share of wine.

"Evening, sir," the motley-appearing bartender greeted as Boyden entered. "Something I can do for you?"

"Ale, my good man," Boyden answered, sending

a glance around the place. His eyes fell on a trio of scantily dressed young women, and he turned to find the bartender placing an ale on the counter.

The man's eyes met Boyden's, and he smiled. "Aye, and they are as fine as they seem, guv'nor. Should you care to spend a moment with any of the three, it could be arranged."

Boyden shook his head and grasped the end of the bar as if in danger of falling. "Not I, friend. If the tall gentleman with the coal-black eyes who only a moment ago left here is an example, I think I will search for a woman who will leave less of a frown on my features."

A puzzled expression took the bartender for a long moment, then suddenly he nodded. "Aye, now I place the one you mean. It's not likely he'd be using one of the girls, seeing as their pay is his. His frown is forever a portion of him. Take your ale, if you wish, and speak with any of the three. But a moment of that and you'll know they'll leave no frown on any face once they set about their task."

Boyden allowed himself to reel back slightly and again look at the girls. "There's not the strength in me to traipse over the town to wherever their lodgings are. It would do me little good to speak with them."

A chuckle of obscenity escaped the bartender's lips. "And you have no problem, there, sir. The girls lodge themselves at the top of the stairs there. You do yourself an injustice if you do not consider them."

Reeling slightly, Boyden again clutched the bar and withdrew his watch. Bringing it close to his face, he peered at it in a drunken manner. When he had studied the dial for a long second, he replaced the watch in its pocket and faced the bartender. "I would have the one with the yellow hair waiting for me in thirty minutes. I must visit my solicitor and claim the five hundred pounds he holds for me." Tipping the ale to his lips, he drained it, taking note of the new light in the other man's eyes at the mention of the money. When he placed the empty tankard on the counter and dropped a coin beside it, he said, "Have her waiting when I return, sir." Then in a stagger he made his way to the door and departed.

Behind him the bartender smiled broadly and called to the blond woman. When she approached the bar, he said, "Get yourself together, Chloe. The one who just now left is at this moment on his way to bring us five hundred pounds. It is you he wishes to relieve him of its weight."

"If he returns," the woman said.

"Ah, I have a feeling he will. He has the look of a man too long without a woman. The special drink will be sent up within minutes of the time he enters your room. If you are about your actions, there will be no necessity of your entertaining him at all. He will return within thirty minutes, if he does not fall and break his wealthy neck on the way."

"Let us pray for his safe being, then," she answered. "I had best see to the bed." Turning, she left the bar and made her way up the stairs.

Full darkness was on the land when Brett hailed a carriage and returned to the Red Boar Inn. His thoughts were on the information he had gleaned from the bartender. When he was delivered to the inn, he paid the driver and made his way to his room, telling himself that there was more to Mr. Currante than anyone suspected.

CHAPTER FIFTEEN

When the evening meal had been completed, the duchess took herself from the room to her quarters, leaving Melissa and her parents to their own devices. Shortly after she had gone, Brinsley stood also, saying, "Well, though I fail to see the attachment she has for this Boyden fellow, I am glad Grandmama has come to her senses concerning Ashley. Ladies, shall we retire to the parlor? I would enjoy a note or two from the spinet, Melissa."

Recalling her great-grandmother's warning about irritating her father, Melissa smiled, saying, "Very well, Father. And will you and Mother lend your voices to the tune?"

A relaxed atmosphere taking them, the three made their way to the parlor to complete the evening. A full hour later Melissa stood to step away from the spinet. "I really must take to my bed, Father. Like Grandmother, I feel the effects of the day. She is not easy to keep abreast of."

Her father smiled sympathetically and nodded in understanding. After kissing both her parents on the cheek, the girl made her way up the stairs to her room. That night her dreams were filled with Brett Boyden.

When the morning sun awakened her and she made her way downstairs, her father and mother were already at breakfast. Taking her place at the table, she asked, "And is Grandmother still abed?"

Brinsley popped a final piece of bread into his mouth. "Ah, would that she was. She awaited me as I came down the stairs. She wished to remind me of the two invitations that are to be tendered this day." Wiping his mouth with a napkin, he stood. "I must be off to the business if I am to do all that is required of me."

"Do you know a method of contacting Mr. Boyden, Reginald?" Lady Brinsley asked.

He snorted shortly and nodded. "It seems the man has taken quarters at a place known as the Red Boar Inn. Grandmama was quick to name his location when she insisted that he be invited for dinner." He shrugged and added, "Well, at least she has taken Ashley in a new light." Then with a nod to his wife and daughter he left.

Lady Brinsley studied her daughter momentarily. "Your father finds pleasure in the fact that the duchess has realized Ashley Currante's worth, Melissa. It would serve you well also if you were to reevaluate his position. He could, I believe, be made to take an interest in you as a wife."

The statement took the girl by surprise. She

held back the angry retort that came to her lips and instead said, "I doubt that he would wish me for a wife, Mother. However, even if such was the case, I cannot find it in me to think of him as a husband to myself."

Her mother's mood did not change. "You would do well to discuss it with your great-grandmother, Melissa. You have ever listened to her recommendations, and I sense that she finds much in Mr. Currante to admire."

Again Melissa held her tongue, only nodding in answer. She was glad when minutes later her breakfast was served and she could place her attention on the food before her.

As she began eating, her mother said, "Well, I must see to the preparations for the evening meal. I would have the occasion much more pleasant than when your grandmother first met Ashley." She left the table and was nearly at the door when she turned to add, "Your grandmother has returned to her room. She asks that you attend her there when you have finished your breakfast."

The words added speed to the girl's eating, and in minutes she was away from the table and hurrying up the stairs to the duchess's room.

"Come in, child," the duchess called when she rapped.

"Good morning, Grandmother," Melissa said happily as she stepped into the room. She stopped then and studied the old woman. Finally she said,

"You are dressed to go out, Grandmother. Is it possible you go to speak with Brett again?"

The duchess chuckled. "Ah, child, your hopeful tone is the reason I am so dressed. I suspected the day would be one of unbearable waiting for you, knowing Brett is to be here this evening. So I have decided this is the day we shall visit the shops and see to the purchase of a new gown for you. I would have you appearing your best when our visitors call."

Happiness showed on Melissa's face. "Oh, Grandmother," she said, moving to throw her arms around the woman. "You are such a splendid person. I shall hurry and change." With that she was out of the room, running down the hall.

"Children in love," the duchess said with a shake of her head.

Reginald Brinsley arrived at his office to find Currante already at work on the day's preparations. Removing his coat and hat, he called to the man and took a seat at his desk.

"Yes, Sir Brinsley?" Currante asked, entering the office.

"Ah, Ashley," Brinsley smiled, "it would seem your generosity and loyalty has struck deep within my grandmother's senses. She wishes you to attend dinner with us this very evening. It is a mark in your favor, for she seldom alters her first impressions."

Currante stood for a second without speaking. Then, a new light entering his eyes, he bowed slightly, saying, "I am honored that the duchess should ask me, sir. I will be pleased to attend dinner with you. And, sir, though it might not be the proper time for such a thing, I would speak with you of Melissa."

"Melissa?" Brinsley asked. "What of her?"

Currante colored slightly and dropped his glance. "Sir, though it has been my intent to do so for some time, I feel now is the opportune moment. I would, if it meets with your approval, speak my troth to Melissa."

The words brought Brinsley's eyes open. He sat for a moment, as if unable to speak. Then, a broad smile taking his face, he stood to come around the desk and offer a hand to Currante. "I had no idea you had even considered such an action, Ashley," he said. "Of course you have my permission. Why, no one could ask for a finer businessman as a son-in-law. Both Lady Brinsley and I will be happy to receive you as a member of the family."

Relief was apparent on Currante's face. "There is nothing to say that she will accept such an offer of marriage from me, sir. But I feel I must make the attempt."

"But why would she not, man? You are intelligent, and you always look to the future."

Currante shrugged. "She ever refers to the difference in our ages, sir. And she has not to this moment expressed any desire to be in my company, either by word or action."

"Bah! She is a child. We shall see that she is advised to look toward the best for her future. Though young, she is not without brains. She will receive your proposal as anyone of sound mind would. Mark my words."

"Thank you, sir," Currante answered. "I wanted to speak of this the night of the demonstration, but the appearance of your grandmother and the words that followed caused me to hold my tongue. It is only your statement that she asked I be invited to the house that causes me to say anything at this moment."

"No matter what the reason, you have my blessing, my boy. Melissa would be a fool to do anything but accept you."

"Thank you, sir. Has there been any word from the authorities on the finances that were stolen from the business?"

Brinsley shook his head. "Nothing more. But you should be forewarned that Grandmother intends to question you concerning your offer of a loan. It is her way. There is nothing I can do to stop her, short of refusing to have you for dinner."

Currante chuckled softly. "I admire the duchess for her caution in financial matters. I, myself, would react similarly to someone with whom I was not acquainted. I shall be happy to answer her questions to the best of my ability. I fear, however, that there is little I can tell her. My friend has insisted he remain unnamed in the transaction, if it is to take place."

Brinsley nodded. "I understand. I only hope Grandmother will understand as well. She asked of the cost of the loan, and I informed her that you would not allow this friend of yours to over-charge me. She trusts no one, I fear."

"And wisely so, sir, for business is business. However nothing has been said between my friend and me of the loan except that the money is available. Any details will have to be decided on by him once a decision is made as to whether or not his help is desired."

"Of course. Of course," Brinsley said. "I informed Grandmother that I would prefer to take a loan from you rather than from that Colonist Boyden. The man does not have the look of one who has the business sense necessary to produce such a sum at any rate."

Currante's eyes narrowed at the statement. "Boyden has made such an offer, sir?"

"Yes," Brinsley nodded. "However, it would require that he go to the United States to raise the money. It would be far past the moment necessary by the time he returned. Besides, as I told Grandmother, I would as leave do business with some-one I know and trust." He paused, then added, "I feel that in the end she will arrange for the sum without the necessity of a loan from anyone. She has ever managed such things to the amazement of all."

"And may she have good fortune in doing so, sir," the representative answered, his mood thoughtful.

Brinsley turned from him to return to the desk, then stopped. "Oh, yes, Grandmother insists that Boyden be invited to dinner also. See to having a messenger contact the man at the Red Boar Inn, if you will."

The "Certainly" was some time in coming from Currante. Then he returned to his desk.

At his desk Brinsley sat thinking of the request made by his employee. Suddenly he laughed shortly and in a pleased manner muttered, "Ashley and Melissa. They will made a striking couple."

CHAPTER SIXTEEN

For the second time Boyden found himself on the Brinsley front stoop at precisely seven o'clock. As he lifted the knocker to rap, a carriage drew to a stop at the stoop and Currante stepped from it. The two men's eyes met and held for a long moment, then Currante turned to pay the driver.

"Mr. Currante, I presume," Boyden said when the other man came even with him.

"And you are, I believe, Mr. Boyden of the Colonies," Currante returned, his black eyes looking down on the shorter man. "It seems we are to be dinner partners this evening."

"Indeed it does," Boyden agreed. "And in the presence of three lovely ladies."

Currante was saved the need to comment on the statement by the opening of the door. Stepping aside, he allowed Boyden to enter ahead of him and, with a nod to the butler, relinquished his hat and coat. Boyden was removing his own coat when Brinsley came into the foyer.

"Ah, Ashley," Brinsley exclaimed, his hand extended to the taller man. "Welcome to Brinsley House." When he had shaken hands with Currante, he gave his attention to Boyden for a moment and nodded, "Mr. Boyden, welcome. Grandmother will be down shortly." He took Currante by the arm and led him toward the parlor.

Boyden chuckled softly as he handed his coat to the butler. Then, a smile on his lips, he stepped along the hallway after the other two. He was nearing the door of the parlor when the duchess called to him from the staircase. Turning, he bowed slightly, saying, "Carrie, you are ravishing. Were it not for your great-granddaughter, I believe I should kidnap you and make you mine."

Gaining the ground floor, she accepted his arm, a smile taking her old lips. "And are you as affected as Charlie is, Brett? If so, it would serve you well to talk with him and accompany him to the nearest medical facility." She paused then, as if only that moment noticing that he was unaccompanied in the hall. "And was there no one to meet you when you entered, Brett?"

He chuckled again and nodded. "Your grandson did, in a manner, greet me and made me welcome. He seemed unduly eager to share Mr. Currante's company rather than mine."

"Total ass," she breathed. "My apologies for his lack of manners, Brett. Though I know it makes not the least whit of difference to you, it is unseemly of him."

Boyden laughed aloud at the statement. "Pray, do not concern yourself, Carrie. Men like him are in this world for a purpose, I'm sure. Do not allow irritation at your grandson to come between you and your purpose this night."

She sobered at the words. "It shall not. Have you seen this Currante person?" And at his nod she added, "What is your opinion now that you have viewed him as other than a rival for Missy?"

Stepping away with her on his arm, he said, "I have always believed that the truth of a man's character shows in his eyes, Carrie. Though it must be taken into consideration that I am prejudiced, his eyes leave me wondering exactly when he will slip the knife into my back."

She nodded. "Well, we shall see. Come, let us join the others." Her glance went down to him then, and the beginning of a smile pulled at her lips. "You have not asked of Missy. Can it be that you have regretted your words and actions toward her?"

The question brought a laugh from him. "Hardly that, Carrie. No, I assumed there was a reason for your not mentioning her. I can only believe that she wishes to make an entrance. If such is the case, I find myself taken with impatience, for she can hardly become more lovely than the last moment I saw her."

The smile became full blown on the old woman's face. "You tend to read people much too closely for their comfort, Brett. Yes, she is now preparing to don a new gown and make her way

164

down the stairs in hopes that you will find her attractive."

"She wastes much time," he told her as they neared the parlor door. "She would be attractive if dressed in the rags of a beggar."

The duchess was still chuckling at the statement when they entered the parlor and faced the three persons gathered there. She paused, her grip on Boyden's arm tightening. Her green eyes moved to take in Lord and Lady Brinsley and their guest, and she said, "It is truly a fortunate day when friends can gather to enjoy each other's company. Mr. Currante, how nice to see you."

Currante had gotten hastily to his feet at her entrance. At her notice of him he moved forward and bent over the hand she offered. "My thanks for your invitation, Duchess," he said, straightening.

"You are quite welcome, Mr. Currante," she returned. "Reginald informs me that an apology is due you for my words at our earlier meeting. I can only say the trip had tired me beyond common limits."

The coal-black eyes met the sharp green ones and held for a moment. Then with a nod Currante said, "It is nothing, your Grace. My only thought was that I had somehow displeased you. I would not care to do that."

She accepted the words with a sober expression.

Then her glance went to her escort and she said, "Brett, I'd like you to meet Mr. Currante. Mr. Currante, a fine friend of mine, Mr. Brett Boyden."

"We met earlier," Currante said, giving Boyden a slight nod of his head. "Mr. Boyden was present at the demonstration of the walk-along."

Melissa chose that moment to enter the room, wearing soft purple covered with white net. She smiled at her great-grandmother and moved directly toward Brett Boyden. "Brett," she said with an impish smile, "how nice to see you again."

His smile matched hers as he bowed to place his lips on her hand. "You are without doubt the loveliest of the lovely, Melissa. My thanks for having me."

"Hummph!" Brinsley snorted. "Melissa, we do have another guest."

Turning to face an irritated Currante, she smiled, saying, "Of course, Mr. Currante. How nice that you could come to dinner. My, you do look the gentleman this evening."

He bowed from the waist. "Melissa," he said, "as Mr. Boyden has stated, you are beautiful. It is my good fortune to be here this evening."

"Melissa," Lady Brinsley said, "would you play and sing at the spinet for us before dinner?"

Facing her mother, Melissa pleaded, "Pray allow the gentlemen to at least dine before being forced to withstand my sour notes, Mother. Once they have eaten, I shall depend on their sated state to keep them from running away at the first sound from my throat."

Everyone laughed at her words. Then a servant entered the room to announce dinner.

"May I escort you, Melissa?" Currante asked, moving forward.

The look of a trapped animal came into her eyes as she realized that Boyden had her great-grandmother on his arm and that she was bound to perform the normal niceties to all guests. Swallowing back the words of rejection that rose to her lips, she accepted the arm offered her and allowed the representative to lead her to the dining room.

To her dismay Currante led her to a chair and immediately stepped to the one to the right of her. She found herself sitting directly across from Boyden, rather than beside him as she had wished to. Irritation took her for a moment, then after considering the placement, she smiled, realizing that the arrangement was perfect.

Boyden waited until the duchess took her chair before turning to his own. His gray eyes came up to meet Melissa's, and he smiled. The smile left his lips a moment later when he met the stern glance of Currante. "It is a pleasure to have such lovely female companions during a meal, don't you agree, sir?" he asked, taking his seat.

"Of course," Currante said, barely concealing

his irritation. He, too, took his seat and, when the first course was before them, began eating.

"And Mr. Currante," the duchess asked suddenly, "what of this loan Reginald made mention of? Is it true that you are in a position to make such a loan?"

"Not I, your Grace. A friend of mine," he answered. "A friend who accepts my recommendation for such a thing."

She nodded. "I see. And what of the interest that will accompany such a loan? Will it be exorbitant?"

Currante colored slightly before shaking his head. "I hardly think so, your Grace. Though it will, in the very fact that it is a business arrangement, require that interest be paid."

"There is no one at this table who would assume any differently. As you say, it is business and therefore to be handled like a business proposition."

"You need not concern yourself about the interest, your Grace," Currante said with a smile. "I am certain my friend will know exactly what the price of the loan should be. He is adept at financial matters."

The duchess snorted. "I do not concern myself at all. I asked of the interest only because of information I collected today dealing with another source for the needed monies. The rate asked is more favorable than any moneylenders of the city would offer. I must look into it further."

The words had a startling effect on Reginald and Currante. Brinsley stared openmouthed at his grandmother for a long moment before saying, "You made no mention of such a thing before this, Grandmother. Who were you thinking of taking a loan from?"

She smiled at him. "As Mr. Currante says of his friend, the person would as well remain anonymous. Suffice it to say the money is available at a very reasonable rate. I shall consider it." Her glance returned to Currante. "If possible, sir, speak with your friend and determine what the rate shall be if the money is gotten from him. I would prefer to deal where it costs the least amount."

The hard line of the agent's lips did not weaken. He nodded. "Very well, your Grace. I shall speak with him on the morrow."

"Fine," she answered, her eyes meeting her great-granddaughter's questioning look. "We shall then know which source is the best."

The conversation turned to other topics until the final course of the meal was completed. Then, as they all stood to return to the parlor, Brinsley said, "Ah, Melissa, though you have agreed to play at the spinet, it has occurred to me that Ashley is the only one present who has not viewed the gardens in the moonlight. As your grandmother stated, they are beautiful. Why do you not take him through the paths and allow him to see them.

Melissa paled slightly at the request. Her glance went to Boyden, who wore a grimace. She met her grandmother's green eyes and detected the message there. Reluctantly she turned to Currante, saying, "Mr. Currante, would you like to view the gardens of Brinsley House? As Father has said, they are beautiful and it would take us but a few short moments to traverse them."

He bowed, a tight-lipped smile on his face. "It would give me the greatest pleasure to accompany you, Melissa, no matter what length of time it should consume."

Brinsley moved forward to herd his wife, the duchess, and Boyden toward the parlor, leaving Melissa and Currante to themselves.

Turning to Currante, Melissa asked, "Shall we go, sir?"

He nodded and offered his arm. "It strikes me that your refusal to use my given name nears the point of ridiculousness, Melissa. Is it so difficult for you to recognize me as a human being?"

She colored slightly and shook her head. "I am sorry, sir. There are, I fear, people in all walks of life who seem to require the formal name. I find it difficult to think of you as other than Mr. Currante." She took his arm then and led him from the dining room toward the rear of the house.

His chuckle brought her head around. "I have said something to strike at your humorous vein, sir?" she asked as they gained the back steps and made their way to the gardens.

"In light of what is about to happen, Melissa, I must admit that you have given my humor an outlet for the moment."

"And what is it that is about to happen?" she asked, a hint of uncertainty in her voice.

They rounded a bend in the path at that moment and stepped from sight of the house. Coming to a stop, he turned to her and looked down into her moonlit face. "Why, I am about to ask you to become Mrs. Ashley Currante, my dear." He paused as her mouth dropped open and her eyes widened. Then, when she did not or could not answer, he continued, "Just today I asked your father's permission to speak my troth to you. He was, I must say, quite elated in the thought that we were to become relatives."

"It is unbelievable," she got out. "It—"

"Hold," he told her, his hands going to her shoulders. "Make no haste with your answer. I wish you to consider the entire matter for at least the remaining portion of the week. I believe you will see the advantage inherent in such a marriage." He paused, then added, "I am not without decent appearances—or finances. You could do worse than to become my bride."

She stared at him in complete disbelief. Then,

becoming aware of his hands on her shoulders, she attempted to pull back, saying, "It is time for us to return to the house."

His grip tightened and the smile vanished from his face. "Do you find me so repulsive, Melissa?" he asked, bending until his face was near her own.

"I—I find you to be as conceited as Grandmother judged you but a few days ago, sir," she got out. "There is no feeling for you at all in me. I certainly will not become your wife for any reason nor at any time."

A bitter chuckle escaped his lips. Then, suddenly, his left hand released her shoulder and went to the back of her head. He pulled her to him and forced his lips down upon hers in a harsh embrace.

She struggled against his hold. Nausea struck her in the pit of her stomach, and she hit at him with her free hand.

He released her and stepped back, an evil smile on his face. "Ah, they say a hellcat is by far the finest kind of woman for a wife."

She stared at him, her color high, her anger taking her breath. "You—you . . ." she began.

." . . . will be a good husband to you," he finished for her. "Although you will find I have little time for your moods or your childishness."

"I would not have you for a pet on a leash," she burst out. "Your rash actions betray you for the

172

cad you truly are." With that she swung a hand and struck him on the face.

Quick as a snake, he grabbed her wrist and twisted. His smile remained intact and increased as she moaned in pain. Then, pulling her roughly to him, he spoke directly into her face. "Take care, spoiled one. Your father's business is in dire straits. There may yet come a time when I do not sicken you." He pushed her away roughly, adding, "Now, we will return to the house. Should your tongue wag the wrong direction concerning what has taken place in this garden, your father may well pray that his accursed grandmother has indeed found a method for replacing the missing money." With that he stepped away from her toward the house.

After a moment she followed him, her hatred bringing color to her features. She halted when she reached the steps and looked up at him. "You are detestable, sir," she muttered. "Your actions and words this night shall not go unpunished."

"Recall the words I spoke only moments ago, idiot girl," he snarled. "Though you may choose to reject me in marriage, it is your family who will suffer should you mention what has passed between us. I alone control the money your father needs should the duchess find she cannot acquire the amount she speaks of having access to."

The words impressed her through her hatred. Grimacing, she stepped to the door, saying, "I

173

loathe you, sir. And I always shall." Moving past him, she entered the house and moved toward the parlor. She hesitated momentarily at the door of the room, aware of the voices coming from within. Hearing Currante's step behind her, she moved quickly to join her parents and the others.

Boyden's eyes were on her the instant she stepped into the room. Those eyes narrowed suddenly and shifted to fix on Currante. Then, his lips molded into a straight line, he got to his feet, asking, "Has something occurred, Melissa?"

For the tenth portion of a second she would have spat out the entire truth of the happenings in the garden. Then Currante's words came back to her and she glanced toward her parents and the duchess. She shook her head. "No, Brett. I stumbled. In so doing I fear I jerked myself unwisely. I am overtaken with a headache such as I have never before known." Her glance again went to the others, and she added, "I would ask pardon and return to my room, if I may. I truly fear I shall become sick if I remain here."

Brinsley moved forward to take her arm. "Of course, dear girl. I'm certain Ashley understands. Go to your room and rest. I shall have tea sent to you immediately."

With a nod at all present and a quick glance at Boyden, she turned, sobbed once, and made her way from the room.

"It was sudden," Currante said in explanation. "One moment we were enjoying the gardens, the next she had stumbled. Had it not been for my arm on hers, she would have struck the ground."

"Ah, Ashley," Brinsley beamed in gratitude, "it is indeed fortunate you were present. My thanks for your services this night."

Currante nodded. "Your servant, sir," he said. "If there is nothing more to discuss, I would take myself to my quarters and rest. I must rise early on the morrow if I am to speak with my friend about the loan."

"Nonsense," Brinsley answered. "You shall take the time from your work tomorrow morning. I shall await you at the office. And my thanks to your friend, whoever he may be. Though it appears Grandmother has discovered another source, I appreciate his offer."

With a nod to the others present Currante took his leave. When he had gone, Brinsley turned to the duchess, saying, "A prince of a man, Grandmama, you must agree."

"We shall see," she answered, her eyes meeting Boyden's.

Boyden moved forward to bow slightly before Lady Brinsley. "Madam," he said, "I, too, feel it time for me to take my leave. If there is anything Melissa requires that I can provide, you have only to notify me." Straightening, he accepted the duchess's hand, met her eyes, and nodded slightly. "Carrie, there is much I would discuss with you at your earliest convenience."

"I will expect you tomorrow afternoon at one o'clock, Brett," she answered. "And thank you for coming this night."

"The pleasure has been mine," he returned, releasing her hand and turning to Lady Brinsley. "My thanks, madam, for an excellent meal." With a final nod to all of them he left.

Currante stood just off the stoop when Boyden stepped from the house. Turning to face the younger man, he said, "I sensed you would be taking your leave, Boyden. I would speak with you if I may."

Boyden studied the man for a moment before saying, "Of course, Mr. Currante. Shall we walk together? Perhaps we shall be lucky enough to find a carriage for hire."

"Perhaps," Currante agreed, falling in beside Boyden. "You are, I believe, a friend of the duchess, are you not?"

Boyden nodded. "A very good friend. Why do you ask?"

Currante hesitated. "Simply concern for her and my employer, sir. I would not have them err in their acceptance of a loan. The amount is certainly not small. Are you aware of the friend who has made an offer to the duchess?"

Boyden stopped and faced him. "Sir, I am not,"

he said. "However, if such were the case, you can be certain I would not make the information known to you or anyone else without Carrie's permission. Your asking for such private information is unseemly. As a friend of the Brinsleys', I resent it."

A small smile took Currante's lips. Nodding, he said, "Of course. It was rude of me. My apologies." He sent a glance down the street then and announced, "Ah, here is a carriage."

"You may take it for yourself," Boyden told him, anger in his tone. "I believe I shall take of the night air." Turning from the man, he set off along the street at a fast pace.

At the rebuff Currante stood for a moment in silence. Then, his smile broadening, he hailed the carriage and gave the driver directions to The Devil's Pit.

CHAPTER SEVENTEEN

Melissa was sobbing into her pillow when the knock came at her door. Fighting to keep the sadness from her voice, she called, "Who is it?"

"It is I, child," the duchess said, stepping into the room. "I wish to know the cause of the sudden headache that overtook you in the garden."

The girl tried to hide her face from the old woman's gaze but failed. Finally, with a sob and a wipe at her eyes with a fist, she said, "Oh, Grandmother, it was terrible. That—that oaf proposed marriage to me and forced his lips upon mine. When I broke away to tell him my thoughts, he grabbed me and hurt my wrist. He is evil beyond design."

The old woman studied her a moment before asking, "And why did you say nothing of this earlier when you arrived back from the gardens? Why did you fabricate a headache that did not exist?"

"Oh, Grandmother," Melissa sobbed, "he threatened to withdraw the offer of assistance to Father and the business should I make any of it known. He would do such a thing, I know."

"Aye, he would," the duchess agreed. Then with a nod she added, "You did right, child. Though the man deserved to be horsewhipped, worse has befallen others and you shall live through this. It serves us well to know his true stripe at this time, however. I shall, ere your father takes a loan from the man, make this happening common knowledge to everyone in this house."

"He was an animal, Grandmother. I have never been handled in such a manner."

Moving to sit on the bed, the duchess took the girl in her arms and consoled her. "There, there, Missy. The wrist will mend from its hurt, and your soul will likewise mend from its shock. Consider what you have gone through this evening as a service to me and your parents. It is truly fortunate that we have this to present to your father when he prepares to ask for a loan from Currante."

Melissa raised her tearful eyes to scan her great-grandmother's face. "You believe he will proceed with the loan from him after hearing of what has taken place? I cannot believe such a thing. Why, no matter what the interest your friend wishes, I'm certain Father will prefer to deal with him rather than with Mr. Currante."

Slowly the duchess shook her head. "Ah, child, you were in my company the entire day. I spoke to no one you did not see. There is no friend with money to loan. That was a ploy meant to force a lower rate from Mr. Currante. No, it would seem that if we are to borrow the money needed, we will indeed be forced to deal with Mr. Currante."

"I would have spoken to Brett had I but had the chance," Melissa said, sobering. "Though it might have caused nothing but trouble, I would have preferred to speak with him. Like the others, he believes you have access to moneys at a low rate of interest."

The duchess nodded. "I shall clear his mind as to that tomorrow afternoon. As to your speaking with him of what took place between Currante and yourself, I would think several moments on such a thing. It strikes me that Brett would have small patience with someone who had done ill to one he loved. I fear Mr. Currante would awaken to find that he was no longer able to do ill to anyone."

"And he deserves such a thing," the girl said emphatically. "Oh, I wish he were dead."

"Nonsense. You are allowing your heart to rule your senses. True, the man is beyond design, but to wish him dead for nothing more than a stolen kiss is idiocy. Now enough of this. Put your head to your pillow and rest. If you can claim a night's sleep, I shall allow you to be present tomorrow when Brett calls at one o'clock." So saying, she stood and, with a final smile at her great-granddaughter, left the room.

"I wish he were dead," Melissa repeated as the door closed behind the old woman. Then, her thoughts filled with the events that had overtaken her, she lay her head on the pillow to partake of a fitful night's sleep.

Upon his arrival at The Devil's Pit, Currante immediately signaled the bartender and, when he came near, ordered, "I wish three men for tomorrow. Their job is important and must not be bungled. Look well to your choices."

"Aye, sir," the bartender answered. "And what sort of work is it they'll be doing?"

Currante was thoughtful for a moment before saying, "Abduction is to be their trade in this instance. Choose those with brains enough to do a thorough job of it. I'll need quill and paper with which to write a note."

When the materials had been brought to him, he wrote quickly for a few minutes, then studied his efforts. With a satisfied nod of his head he folded the note and handed it to the bartender, saying, "Now, listen closely. This is how the thing must be done."

The sound of horses' hooves brought Melissa from a sound sleep. Stretching, she rose from her bed and crossed to the window to look out upon the drive. She was slightly surprised at the height of the sun and realized that a restful sleep had overtaken her late in the night. She spotted the rider then and wondered at his presence. Then she observed the passing of a paper from him to the butler. She stood watching until the messenger again mounted his horse and left the premises.

She was donning her clothing for the day when the rap came at the door. Moving swiftly to answer the summons, she opened the door and stood face to face with her great-grandmother.

"Good morning, Missy," the old woman said. "I asked that they allow you to sleep your rest out. Do you feel better this morning?"

"I do, Grandmother," Melissa assured her with a nod. "The events of last night are like a terrible dream that I have no desire to relive. What brings you rapping on my door?"

The duchess extended a note to her, saying, "A note from Brett to me. He asks that I meet him before the noon hour at a place called the Willfurd Green. He is sending a carriage for me."

"I shall hurry and complete my toilet, Grandmother," the girl replied, a smile on her face.

"Hold, child. He asks that I come alone. He has undoubtedly discovered something of importance that at the moment he deems for my ears only. I came to tell you of this so you would not be saddened that our meeting with him this afternoon might not occur."

"But, Grandmother, surely he would not mind if I—"

"No, girl. Brett has a head on his shoulders. He would not have asked that I come alone unless there was reason. Lord, are you not aware that he wishes to see you as much as you wish to see him?"

Reluctantly Melissa nodded. "Yes, Grandmother. Of course, you are correct. I would have him know of my desire to see him, though."

The old lady chuckled. "Ah, and he shall, child. Now I must prepare for the carriage." She turned away and made her way to the master guest room.

Melissa stood as she was for several moments, studying the note her great-grandmother had received. Finally, with a sigh of disappointment, she turned to the job of completing her toilet.

The carriage moved swiftly through the streets of London, jarring the duchess with every turn of the wheels. Finally, after a close call with another carriage, the vehicle drew to a stop and the driver opened the door for her, saying, "This way, milady."

She stepped warily into a cluttered alley at the mouth of which sat a blind, legless beggar. Passing his position, she dropped coins into the alms bowl he held in his lap, then followed the driver, her thoughts on the reason for Boyden's choosing this meeting place. As she was about to question the driver of their final destination, he stopped at a doorway and opened the portal. Stepping back, he bowed for her to pass through before him.

With a nod to the man she stepped into the semidark room. "Brett," she called, her eyes unable to pierce the gloom that surrounded her. "Brett," she repeated just before a rough hand clamped her mouth and her arms were pinned to her sides by a grip of steel.

CHAPTER EIGHTEEN

Reginald Brinsley sat in stunned silence at his desk. Before him lay three separate notes from creditors. "Animals," he muttered, considering the demands. A sound from the front of the building came to him, and he looked up to find Currante entering. Relief was obvious in his features when he said, "Ah, Ashley, you return from meeting with your friend."

Currante nodded, a tight smile on his features. "Yes, Sir Reginald. I have spoken with him and the arrangements have been defined. Shall I wait for your grandmother to be present before relating them to you?"

"Lord, no, man," Brinsley exclaimed, grasping the three duns. "Word of my situation is common knowledge, it seems. The birds of prey have begun to strike. Payment is being demanded from every quarter. I would know immediately what your friend requires."

Currante hesitated, then said, "It is the lunch hour, sir. Could I purchase you beef and soup? The telling of the details will serve as well over a meal as at any other time."

"It shall be my pleasure to see to the purchase

of both our meals, Ashley. But, first, the requirements from your friend."

"Very well, sir," Currante said, moving closer to the desk. "Though it comes as some surprise to me, I have no control over the decision. In exchange for lending sixty-two thousand pounds, my friend would have me become a full and equal partner in Brinsley Enterprises."

For a moment it seemed Brinsley had not heard the words. Then his eyes widened and his mouth opened. He gasped once before saying, "Impossible! Brinsley Enterprises has always been totally owned by the family. No! There is no way such a requirement can be brought about."

Currante shrugged, saying, "Then it would seem you must rely on the loan from the duchess's source, sir. I understand your meaning and sympathize. I spoke of it to my friend but he was adamant. Nothing will do for him but that I become a partner. I told him you would not accept such a condition."

The shocked expression seeped from Brinsley's features slowly. Then, wiping at his sweating forehead, he said, "Of course, Ashley, your friend cares for you and attempts to use the loan as a method of improving your station. I cannot find fault with his desire to help a friend. But, as you point out, I must decline and allow the duchess to borrow the money from her source."

186

"As you will, sir," the agent nodded. "Shall we take lunch now?"

"Eh?" Brinsley asked, his thoughts whirling. "Oh, yes. Come. We shall dine, and then I must hie myself to the house and speak with the duchess. All haste must be made in acquiring the money needed. Those who hold portions of my debts will not wait now that word of my situation is out. Come." He came around the desk and led the way from the office.

A satisfied smile rested on Currante's lips as he followed his employer to the street.

It was nearing one o'clock when the Brinsley carriage drew to a stop at the stoop of the house and Brinsley stepped out. He was at the door preparing to enter when a second carriage came into the drive. Turning, he sent a puzzled glance toward the vehicle, muttering. "Now, who can that be at such a time?"

Brett Boyden stepped from the coach and paid the driver. Turning, he noticed Brinsley and nodded. "Good day to you, sir," he said, moving up the steps. "And on a day as lovely as this, there can be little wrong with the world, can there?"

Brinsley nodded, a frown on his features. "It is a fine day, Boyden. What is it you desire at Brinsley House this day?"

Brett chuckled lightly. "The duchess, you will

187

recall, asked that I attend her at this hour. Having received no word to the contrary, I assumed she remained of the same mind."

Recalling the invitation from his grandmother on the previous evening, Brinsley grudgingly nodded. "Oh, yes, Grandmama did ask that you come. If it is not a bother, Boyden, I would delay your meeting with her for a period long enough to apprise her of certain facts. They are, I am certain, of more importance than whatever it is the two of you would discuss."

A smile on his face, Boyden nodded in agreement. "Your servant, Sir Reginald. As you say, our discussion can be of no major importance."

"Very well, then," Brinsley answered shortly, "come along. I shall tell Grandmama you are here."

The smile was still on his face as he followed Brinsley into the house and relinquished his coat to the butler. "Would it be possible for me to speak with Melissa while waiting for the duchess, sir?" he asked.

"Eh, what?" Brinsley asked. "Oh, Melissa. Ah . . . I see no reason why you should not speak with her—in the presence of Lady Brinsley of course."

"Of course," Boyden agreed.

"We shall most likely find the three of them in the parlor. Come," Brinsley said, leading the way down the hall.

Lady Brinsley looked up from her needlepoint as the two men entered the parlor. She smiled at her husband. "Ah, Reginald, you are home early." Her glance shifted to Boyden, and a puzzled expression took her face. "Mr. Boyden," she said, "I—"

At the words Melissa swung from the spinet and rose to her feet. Her eyes were on Brett as she asked, "What of Grandmother, Brett?"

"I would have audience with your grandmother before Mr. Boyden and she see to their plans for the day," Brinsley announced, a frown of irritation on his features.

"But—but, she is not here," Melissa said.

"Not here?" Brinsley demanded. "Then where is she? It is imperative that I speak with her at once."

Melissa's questioning glance was on Boyden. "Grandmother received your note asking that she meet you before the noon hour," she said. "The carriage you sent arrived and left with her hours ago."

"Note?" Boyden asked. "I sent no note to the duchess."

"But you did," the girl said. "I have it in my room. I have read it."

He shook his head with a worried expression. "I sent no note. There is something afoot here that is not right."

"Where was she going?" Brinsley demanded. "Quickly, girl, there is no time to waste."

Melissa, her expression taking on much the worried expression Brett wore, said, "I shall get the note and return, Father. The message is quite clear to anyone who reads it." She left the room and ran up the stairs. Minutes later she was back, extending the note to her father. "The place named is Willfurd Green, Father," she said. "Can it be possible that someone is playing a monstrous joke on Grandmother and us?"

Brinsley read the note silently, then raised his eyes to look at Boyden. Handing the paper to him, he asked, "You did not write this message, sir?"

Accepting the note, Boyden studied it for a long moment before shaking his head. "I did not, sir. It is obviously a forgery. The question is, why has the forgery been made and where is the duchess at this moment?"

"Where indeed?" Brinsley echoed. "I must speak with her at once. I must."

Boyden was thoughtfully silent. He stood as if separated from the others by an invisible wall. Suddenly his eyes brightened and he said, "I fear the duchess may be in danger, sir. There can be no other reason for such a thing as the note and the carriage."

"Nonsense," Brinsley snapped. "Who in their right mind would wish harm to her?"

"That I cannot tell you, sir, but I believe I shall

190

go to this Willfurd Green and attempt to locate her." Turning, he made his way to the front of the house.

"Brett," Melissa called, moving swiftly to his side. "Brett, what can it mean? Who would wish Grandmother harm? Where can she be at this moment?"

He smiled reassuringly. "Do not concern yourself, Melissa. Though I am certain there is something amiss, there would be no reason for anyone to harm your grandmother. I shall return with news of her shortly." He was about to step from the room when the butler entered to hand Brinsley a note.

Opening the note, Brinsley perused it for a long moment. His features became ashen, and he snapped his head up to send a harsh glance at Boyden. "You, sir, are of a cunning beneath anyone I know."

The statement took Boyden by surprise. He stared at the man for several seconds before asking, "And what brings you to such a conclusion, sir?"

Extending the note, the older man snarled. "Your plot will do you no good, sir. The authorities will deal harshly with you for this act."

Taking the note, Boyden read it and then handed it to Melissa. Facing her father, he said, "I sympathize with your feelings, sir, but this is none of my doing. It is not I who have laid pen to paper with the demands of ransom for the duchess."

"Liar!" Brinsley exclaimed. "The two notes are in the same hand. Do you take me for an idiot?"

"Father," Melissa said, laying a hand on his arm. "Brett would not so such a thing. True, the notes are in similar hands, but there is nothing to say that Brett wrote either one of them. You do him an injustice."

"We are wasting valuable time, sir," Boyden said, his glance steady on Brinsley. "I would suggest we put our thoughts to methods of accomplishing the return of the duchess rather than waste them in accusations that have no basis."

Frowning, Brinsley turned to Melissa. "Writing materials, Melissa, immediately. We shall allow Mr. Boyden the opportunity to write the words contained in the two notes. Then we shall know if he has instigated this horrible deed."

She stood as if paralyzed. Then, her eyes filling, she said, "Oh, Father, you err in your judgment. Brett would do nothing to harm Grandmother. As he has stated, you spend time accusing him while Grandmother is indeed in the danger he supposed. Father, she has been abducted. Can't you—"

"Enough, Melissa," Boyden said. "Get the materials your father asked for. It will serve to ease all your minds when I do as he suggests. Hurry, girl. There is no time to waste."

Brinsley's expression softened at the younger

man's words. He hesitated, then said, "If it is true that I have accused you unjustly, I will apologize, sir. I will require the writing from your hand, though. I know of no others of the duchess's recent acquaintance and therefore must suspect you."

Boyden nodded. "Understandable, sir, and no apologies are needed. The important thing is that we save Carrie from whoever has her. Can you think of any reason why such a thing should be performed at this time?"

Brinsley shook his head. "The deed has been proposed by one who is not aware of the facts, obviously. The demand for twenty thousand pounds at this time is illogical for anyone who knows of my position."

Boyden nodded and refrained from making mention of the fact that he was completely aware of Brinsley's position. Melissa returned to the parlor at that moment bearing the writing materials. Immediately Brett moved to take the paper and quill from her. Seating himself at a table, he penned the exact messages of the two notes and handed them to Brinsley, saying, "Your judgment, sir."

"Of course," Brinsley said, accepting the papers. He moved to the window and, with the notes and the copies in hand, studied them carefully. Finally, a defeated expression on his face, he turned to the others. "I seem to have miscalculated, Mr.

Boyden. My apologies. Your hand is nothing like the one that penned these notes. My God, I am ruined."

"Father!" Melissa exclaimed. "How can you think of yourself at such a moment?"

"True, Reginald," Lady Brinsley interjected. "To speak of your ruin at this moment when the duchess is in danger for her life is unkind."

"You refer to the loan from your man Currante, sir?" Boyden asked. "Though the twenty thousand pounds nears a third of the amount you ask, the remaining will surely prevent the ruin you speak of."

Brinsley eyed him suspiciously. "You seem privy to the closest secrets of this family and its business, sir. How are you aware of these things?"

"Oh, Father," Melissa interrupted, "Grandmother has discussed the situation fully with Brett. It was on that occasion that he offered a loan to assist you. She spoke to you of the offer, if you will recall." Color flooded her face then, and her lips drew into an angry line. "Why do we stand here mouthing nonsense? Someone must do something to save Grandmother."

Boyden placed a hand on her arm. "Ease yourself, Melissa. Your father is distraught with Carrie's situation, as we all are. He means nothing by his statements." Turning back to Brinsley, he asked, "And the forty-odd thousand pounds that will remain after the ransoming of the duchess, sir—if it will not be sufficient to soothe your creditors, I shall be happy to speak with them of further payment. It will require only that I be allowed to return to the United States and collect the amount necessary."

Brinsley sagged visibly. "Ah, there is no loan from Currante, I fear. Only an hour ago I refused the offer of a loan from his friend."

"Would it not be possible to recall the refusal, sir?" Boyden asked.

Brinsley shook his head. "I fear that is not possible. The rate of interest demanded was unacceptable. But even so I would forgo half of the business to ransom Grandmama. But I fear that now Ashley has reported my refusal to his friend." He became thoughtful for a moment, then added, "I shall leave immediately to search out Ashley. Possibly he may speak with his friend and, as you suggested, sir, allow me to recall my refusal."

Melissa stepped to her father's side. "You spoke of the interest, Father. What payment was beyond agreement?"

Brinsley glanced at his wife, then at Boyden. "The man demanded that Ashley become a full partner in Brinsley Enterprises as interest payment for the loan. It was, at the time, preposterous, and I informed Ashley of that fact. Now, however, it seems the only way to save Grandmama and to hopefully stave off my creditors. I must hasten in search of Ashley. The ransom demand requires that the money be paid by tomorrow." He turned and made as if to leave.

This information held the other three in stunned silence for a long moment. Then, clearing his throat, Boyden asked, "And Mr. Currante's feelings concerning the demands of his friend, sir. What were they?"

Brinsley shrugged. "While Ashley—being the forward-looking person he is—would have cared for a position as full partner, he admitted he was surprised by the demand."

"And when you refused such an offer?" Boyden pressed.

"Why, he simply stated that it would seem I must rely on the source known by Grandmama for the needed money. It is the reason I would have spoken to her on the instant of my arrival here. And now there is no way. . . ." He paused then, his glance going to Melissa. "Missy, is it possible you know the identity of the financier your grandmother mentioned last evening?"

Tears filled the girl's eyes. She shook her head, saying, "Oh, Father, there was no other source. Grandmother spoke of such a thing in an attempt to drive down the cost of the loan from Mr. Currante."

"What?" her father exclaimed. "No other source? My God, then there is no choice. I must allow Ashley to become full partner in the business." His expression saddened. "For the first time the Brinsley Enterprises will be shared with one not of the family."

"Convenient," Brett muttered, bringing all eyes to him.

"What did you say, sir?" Brinsley asked.

"Only thinking aloud, sir. It occurs to me that the abduction of the duchess falls at a very convenient time to force you into giving up half of your business to Currante in payment for the loan. It could mean nothing, but—"

The red of anger swept over Brinsley's features. "Are you, sir, suggesting that Ashley has had a hand in the abduction of my grandmother? That is utter nonsense. Granted, it places me in a position I do not favor, but Ashley would never play a part in such a scheme."

"He *is* capable of such a thing, Father," Melissa interjected.

He turned to face her. "And how can you say such a thing, Missy? Why, only yesterday he asked permission to speak his troth to you. Can you believe a man who wishes you for a bride would do such a thing to one you hold dear?"

"He holds only himself and wealth dear, Father. He detests Grandmother with a passion." Her eyes went to Boyden. "He is a user of women and all other things that would assist him toward his ends."

Boyden's eyes narrowed. "Something has taken place, Melissa," he said. "What is it?"

"Mr. Currante offered for my hand while we walked in the garden last night. When I refused him, he forced his will on me and later threatened to see to a refusal of the loan if I should mention his actions to anyone."

"Ashley?" Brinsley demanded. "I cannot believe such a thing. He would never—"

"He never shall again," Boyden interrupted, his eyes narrowed, his mouth set in a straight line of anger. Turning from them, he again began to leave the room.

"Hold, Boyden," Brinsley called. "Though I find it difficult to believe such a thing of Ashley, it could be so. However this is not the time to take him to task for his shortcomings. I fear we are in need of his goodwill at this moment."

"I, sir, am in need of nothing from the man," Boyden snapped.

"But my family and I are, sir," Brinsley answered, a glance of appraisal in his eyes. "I sense there is that between Melissa and yourself that amounts to more than mere friendship. If you have feelings for her at all, sir, you will restrain yourself, lest she suffer along with the rest of Brinsley Enterprises."

Boyden met the girl's eyes and read a message there. He nodded shortly. "Very well, sir. Secure your loan and your new partner. I shall wait until

Currante is beyond harming you or yours. At this moment I shall take myself to this Willfurd Green and attempt to locate the duchess from that point. Good luck with your business dealings." On that note he turned and left.

CHAPTER NINETEEN

The duchess sat in total discomfort in the dark and smelly room. Hours earlier she had been brought there in bonds, blindfolded, gagged, and had been tied to the uncomfortable chair and left alone. The last thing she had heard was the door being bolted as her captors left. Now, mentally cursing the gag and blindfold, she set her mind on a means of escape. From all around her room she could hear the rustle of human movement. She hoped that someone would venture into the room and find her trussed.

She was thus engrossed in thought when the rasping sound of the bolt being moved caught her attention. Moments later the sounds of someone entering the room became apparent. She stiffened, awaiting whatever her fate was to be.

"And so this is the overbearing one who considers all others trash, is it?" a voice she thought familiar said. "Well," it continued, drawing closer, "it seems one of the titled class has this day taken a fall from her pillar."

Recognition of the voice came to her then, and she struggled against the restraining bonds that held her to the chair. She sensed the man's presence next to her. The next moment hands were working at the knot that held the blindfold over her eyes. When the blinding cloth fell free, she jerked her head around and stared into the hatred-filled eyes of Ashley Currante.

A bitter smile taking his lips, he bowed mockingly. "Welcome, your grace, to my establishment."

She mumbled viciously against the outrage done her and received only a vicious chuckle from the man in answer. He stepped back a pace as her efforts continued, and after several moments of watching her useless struggles, he stepped forward again in a threatening manner.

"So, I am the idiot your grandson hires as representative, am I?" he asked. His palm came forward to take her across the cheek, driving her head around to its limits. "It is your grandson and all related to him who are idiots, madam."

The green eyes were damp with pain when she brought her head back to stare at him. She mumbled angrily around the gag and again strained against her bonds, all to no avail.

"Ah, you would speak with me, would you?" Currante asked. "Very well, I shall remove the gag that quiets your acid tongue and allow you to thank me for an experience I'm sure is new to you." So saying, he stepped behind her and began working at the knots. As his fingers undid the tie, he added, "Should you choose to scream or yell, it will do you no good. You, madam, are within the confines of a brothel—my brothel bought with Brinsley funds. There is no one on the premises who will dare to enter the room to find what your alarm means." The gag's pressure released as he finished the statement.

For several seconds she worked her jaws and her tongue to offset the unpleasantness caused by the gag. Then, the soreness diminishing, she said, "You, sir, have performed the most asinine deed of your life. You are from this moment destined to die in prison for your foul deeds."

His laugh filled the room. Moving to take a chair across the room from her, he said, "Why, your Grace, how you do rave on." The smile left his face then, and he snarled. "It is not prison that I shall receive for my actions, old hag. Within a matter of hours I shall become a full partner in Brinsley Enterprises."

"Are you insane as well as a thug, sir?" she demanded. "Are you so besot as to think that Reginald or any other friend or relative of mine will allow you to succeed in this coercion?"

The bitter laugh came again, and a new light entered the evil black eyes. "I do, indeed, madam. Your words have brought to mind another slight offered to me by the Brinsley tribe. The spoiled snip of a granddaughter you so love will, I am certain, see fit to join me in marriage when it becomes clear that your very existence depends on her actions. Yes. Yes, that will be the final reward for my hours of slavery to your grandson."

"You are mad, sir. Once I am free of these bonds, the authorities will see to your confinement for the rest of your life. Nothing you gain from this will avail you profit."

He fixed her with a stare, a harsh smile on his face. Then he took a small pistol from his pocket and pointed it at her, saying, "You jest, your Grace. Do you believe you shall leave this room alive? Surely you realize I am of more intelligence than that. As to the profit of this thing, as I stated, this brothel was purchased with Brinsley funds. The other missing moneys now lay in safety at my place of lodging."

"You are mad," the duchess said. "How can you possibly hope to succeed in such an endeavor? Even now the officials have been alerted to my disappearance and are searching the city for my whereabouts. I suggest you release me so that it might go easier on you."

He shook his head as if reasoning with a child. "Ah, madam, you border on complete stupidity. At this moment your grandson and loved ones are considering the ransom demands for your safe return. There can be no alternative for them but to accept any terms I set forward to save the business and to effect your return. No, madam, I am in control of the situation at present. The station I deserve shall be mine within but a few hours."

Her green eyes narrowed at his words. She swiftly considered the significance of the statement and said, "You mistake all the Brinsley family, sir. They realize my age and that I have few years left to me on this earth. They will never allow such a thing as you suggest."

"We shall see, shan't we?" he answered, getting to his feet and returning the pistol to his pocket. "Yes, we shall see. At this moment, unless I misguess, your grandson is searching for me to renew his efforts to acquire the loan. I shall replace your gag and return to the business." He moved to do so, adding, "Once my demands are met, I shall return to inform you of the weakness of your tribe, your Grace. At that moment you would do well to make your peace with God." He knotted the gag tightly and stepped in front of her to bow again. "Your servant, madam." Then, turning, he left the room and threw the bolt.

Behind him the duchess raised her eyes to the heavens and offered a silent prayer for salvation.

CHAPTER TWENTY

Upon leaving the Brinsley house, Brett Boyden hailed a rental carriage and gave the Willfurd Green name to the driver. "And make all haste, my good man," he added.

The driver studied him, taking in the fine boots and quality dress. With a shake of his head he answered, "If that's your wish, sir." Cracking the whip, he sent the horses into motion.

"What is it about my request that concerns you, man?" Brett asked.

"It's naught to me, sir," came the answer, "but it does seem a bit early in the day for one of your caliber to be entering such a neighborhood."

"And where is this neighborhood? I've only moments ago heard of it."

The driver pulled the carriage to a stop and turned. "Then, you'll not want to be going there, sir. There's nothing there but the dregs of humanity. They'd as soon slit your throat for the polished boots you wear as look at you."

Boyden considered the information and finally nodded. "From your description it seems that the place is exactly as I had imagined it would be.

Fear not for my welfare, sir, though I thank you. I would be taken to Willfurd Green immediately."

With a shake of his head, which spoke volumes, the driver again applied whip to horses, and the carriage moved away swiftly.

Some twenty minutes later, it drew to a stop and Boyden stepped from it, saying, "I would ask that you wait, if possible. I seek only information here and it should take no longer than half an hour."

"Aye, sir," answered the driver. "I shall wait and be available if you should need me. The Willfurd Green you asked for is this alleyway, bordered on both sides by groups of buildings." He hesitated, then added, "The alleyway itself is an invitation to all forms of dire things. I doubt that I need go into them, since you would not otherwise have reason for entering there."

With a nod and a smile Boyden said, "And again I thank you, sir. I shall return shortly. Have yourself ready to leave at a moment's notice." With that he turned and entered the alley called Willfurd Green.

Upon entering the alley, he instantly noted a legless, blind beggar who sat against one wall pleading for alms. With a glance around him at the others present in the filthy alley, he crossed to the beggar and said, "It strikes me you are ever at this spot, sir. Am I correct?"

"Always" was the answer. "From the early morn

206

when my son brings me here, till the late night when he comes to return me to our poor dwelling. Would you have ha'penny for one such as I, sir?"

"I seek information and am willing to pay for it," Boyden told him. "Earlier this same day a lady of more than six feet in height, with green eyes and regal bearing, entered this alley in the company of at least one man. Have you noted such a person?"

"Ah, sir, do you make jest of a poor blind beggar? The bandages you see cover but the sockets of what were at one time the sharpest of eyes. I would be of assistance, but it is impossible. Can you find it in your heart to give to a needy soul?"

Drawing his wallet from a pocket, Boyden thumbed out several pound notes and held them toward the beggar, saying, "If you are as you say, I cannot fathom the reason for the small, nearly invisible holes within the bandage. If you are, as I believe you to be, a beggar of standing with the best, you will earn that which I hold before you."

For an instant the beggar was silent. Then the lips below the bandage spread into a smile, and he reached to take the money from Boyden's hand.

Pulling his hand back, Boyden said, "I said you would earn the money, sir. I seek information on the whereabouts of the lady I mentioned."

"Aye," the beggar said. "It was but a short while ago she stepped into the alley from the same spot as you. Her hair was the aged gray and she walked with a pride in her bearing that I have seldom seen the match of."

"And?" Boyden prodded.

"And the lady was generous to a fault, sir. Unlike yourself, she had not the time to notice the sight holes in the bandage. She dropped coins into my bowl as if by habit. Had it not been for my supposed blindness, I would have spoken to her of the danger within these walls."

Boyden's interest quickened at the words. "Tell me, sir, did you take note of where in this maze she made for?"

"Number eight was her destination, sir. She entered there when the gentleman with her ushered her through the door."

Boyden handed the pound notes to him. "My thanks, sir. Perhaps I am not yet too late." Turning, he went in search of number eight.

"Hold," came the call from behind him.

"Sir?" he asked, returning to the beggar.

"If you search for the lady we discussed, you'll not find her there, I'm thinking. It was but a short time after her entry of number eight that her escort and three others came from the place under the burden of a large box. The box was of a length and breadth to hold one such as the lady you ask of."

His nerves tensing, Boyden asked, "And is it known to you where they were bound with the box, sir?"

"They spoke not at all in my hearing," came the answer. "Their deed and destination are unknown to me."

Extracting several more notes from his wallet, Boyden handed them to the man, asking, "And who or what occupies number eight of this alley?"

"There is no one at present, sir," the beggar told him. Then his voice dropped. "There are, however, three of the alley's worst at your back this moment."

The final word of warning had not passed the beggar's lips when Boyden spun on a heel to come face to face with three burly, unshaven men. A knife in the hand of the nearest and the short clubs of the other two left little question as to their intent.

"You wish an audience with me, gentlemen?" Boyden asked, his body loose, his eyes steady on the three.

"Audience?" the knife wielder asked. "It is the fat wallet you only a moment ago dropped into your pocket we have need of, my fine dandy."

A chuckle escaped Boyden's lips. The gray of his eyes became flint hard, and he said, "Ah, my stay in London has until this moment been without proper exercise." He bowed slightly, adding, "The wallet in question is yours, gentlemen. You have but to take it."

"And so we shall," the holder of the knife exclaimed, lunging forward.

Swift as an attacking leopard, Boyden's hand streaked forward to grip the wrist of the assailant. The next instant, the well-polished toe of his boot settled harshly in the groin of the man, dragging an oath of pain from him. Then, Boyden's free hand folded into a fist, he struck at the man's nape.

The remaining two thugs stopped in their tracks as their cohort sunk to the alley floor, his face contorted in pain, his breath coming in heavy gasps.

"Well, gentlemen?" Boyden asked calmly.

The two exchanged glances. Taking a step to the rear, the larger told his comrade, "He's done for the bloke, no question. It's my thought easier prey will surface. I want no part of this one, no matter how thick the wallet appears."

The second man retreated also, his club held at the ready, his eyes on the small man who had in the wink of an eye felled their comrade. Suddenly both men turned and made their way hurriedly away from the site.

"Well done, sir," the beggar chuckled. "It is past time those bully boys learned the lesson you've taught today."

For the third time Boyden drew the wallet from his pocket and removed a sheaf of notes. "Had it not been for your warning, these would now be in the possession of those thugs, sir. My thanks, and may you have a splendid life."

"And to you, sir," the beggar answered, accepting the money. "Go with God. May you find the lady you search for."

The tenseness of battle left Boyden's body as he stepped from the alley and again seated himself in the carriage. He gave directions to the driver and settled back to rally his thoughts of what he had learned. He was in deep concentration when the driver pulled to a stop at the stoop of the Earl of Morgan's house.

After paying the carriage driver, Boyden made his way to the door and rapped. Seconds later the butler opened the door and immediately escorted him into the presence of the earl.

"Boyden," the earl exclaimed upon seeing the American, "and to what do I owe this visit?"

"Ill tidings, sir," Boyden answered. "Carrie has been abducted and a ransom demand has been made upon her grandson for her safe return."

The earl's face became a mask of disbelief. Then with an oath he said, "Come, man, sit and tell me everything. When did this take place and what is known of her abductors?"

In a matter of minutes Boyden had related the facts of the kidnapping to the older man. When he had completed his tale, he said, "It struck me that of all people known to me, Ashley Currante—the one mentioned by Carrie earlier—is in the way of profiting most from this happening. Though I cannot in all good conscience accuse the man, I am suspicious of such coincidence."

The earl nodded thoughtfully. "If it is as you say, you are within your rights to be wary of the man. Now, tell me, what is being done to acquire the money for Carrie's ransom?"

Boyden shrugged. "Brinsley is searching for Currante to borrow the needed money under the man's own terms. With that the ransom can be paid and the business partially saved. I came to you in the hope your man had knowledge of Carrie's whereabouts from his observation of Currante."

The earl turned to consult a mantel clock and said, "You are in luck. His hour of report is within minutes. Let us pray the man has seen something that will direct us to Carrie's place of captivity."

"If he has nothing of value to us, I fear . . ." Boyden began, then ceased speaking as the butler ushered the investigator into the room.

"Ah, man, quickly, give us your report," the earl said, then caught himself. "My apologies, gentlemen. Brett Boyden, this gentleman is the finest investigator in the country. James Parkins, meet Mr. Brett Boyden of America. Now, tell us of your assignment."

The man shrugged. "There is little to tell, sir. As I reported earlier, he goes to the business, his lodgings, and the grog shop known as The Devil's Pit. Other than that, he had lunch with his employer—one Reginald Brinsley—and last evening spent the dinner hour with the Brinsley family."

He fixed Boyden with a glance and added, "This gentleman was present at the Brinsley house on the occasion of last evening, I believe."

Brett nodded in response to the statement. "You say Currante has gone nowhere but his lodgings and The Devil's Pit?"

"Aye, sir," came the immediate answer. "That and the business place."

"Something is amiss, then," Boyden said, his manner thoughtful. "This very morning he called on someone to arrange a loan. He then returned to the business house and met with Brinsley."

"No, sir. Begging your pardon, sir," the investigator corrected. "This morning he did not leave his lodgings until nearing the lunch hour. He then went straight to the business and, a short time after arriving there, left with Brinsley to go to an inn for lunch. Following the lunch, he made his way back to his lodgings, stayed there only a short time, and then went to The Devil's Pit. It was on his leaving the Pit only thirty minutes ago to return to the business house that I deemed it possible to make my report to the earl."

Boyden glanced at the earl. "Is this man as efficient as you say, sir?" he asked. "I mean no disrespect, but this report is of the utmost importance. If what he says is true, then something is truly amiss with this Currante and the imagined friend who wishes to loan Brinsley the needed money."

"He is completely trustworthy, Brett" was the

instant answer. "If he says it, then that is the way it is." He paused, then asked, "What is it you are thinking?"

"I am thinking a visit should be paid to The Devil's Pit. After following your man and Currante to the place, I visited it in the guise of one besot with rum. For all practical purposes it is a brothel of the lowest order. Information I gleaned from the innkeeper leads me to believe that the place is owned by Mr. Currante. If such is the case, then it is possible—nay, probable—that Carrie is being held within the confines of those walls."

An appreciative expression on his features, the earl said, "An excellent bit of investigating, Boyden. Should you, in the future, be in search of work, call on me. Your idea is a valid one. However for you to attempt to enter the place and seek out Carrie is foolhardy."

"Perhaps," Boyden agreed. "But foolhardy or not I intend to do it. If you will pardon me, gentlemen." He turned to leave.

"Not so fast, young man," the earl ordered. "Your concern for Carrie is obvious, but you are not the only one who harbors such feelings. Allow me to get my coat and pistol. Parkins and I shall join you. In the likely event that you will require assistance, we shall be somewhere about, waiting."

"This, I feel, is to be a younger man's game, sir," Boyden pointed out. "I would not have you—"

"Nonsense" was the instant retort. "Carrie is dear to me. Too much of my time these past few years has been spent on my backside. No, with or without your permission, Parkins and I shall be there. It strikes me, we would all benefit from co-operation."

Boyden chuckled and nodded in agreement. "I cannot argue with you, sir. I shall await you. We will settle our plans as we proceed to The Devil's Pit."

CHAPTER TWENTY-ONE

Upon leaving the duchess, Currante made his way to the ground floor, spoke shortly to the bartender, and left The Devil's Pit to return to the offices of Brinsley Enterprises. Only minutes after his arrival Brinsley entered the building hurriedly. An expression of relief swept over the older man's face as he saw the agent.

"Ah, Ashley," he said, "is it possible you have not spoken with your friend concerning the refusal of the loan?"

Currante met his employer's concerned glance with a frown. "Why, sir," he said, "I notified him of your decision only a short while following our lunch. If you are concerned about his feelings in the matter, I assure you you need not worry. It matters little to one such as he if people choose to refuse his offers and terms."

"Yes, of course. However the situation has altered in the extreme. I find myself in need of financing to a point beyond my past needs. Would it be possible for you to contact the man and again secure his generosity to me?"

Currante's expression changed to one of puzzled questioning. "Is something amiss, Sir Reginald? Your manner suggests that something of a vital nature has taken place."

Grimacing, Brinsley nodded. "You are very discerning, Ashley. It is true. Brigands of God-knows-what nature have made off with the duchess. Abducted her, they have. They demand payment of twenty-thousand pounds ransom by tomorrow evening. Without your friend's financing I fear her life will be forfeited."

"Ah, sir, your concern is understandable. I shall hie myself to my friend's residence and speak with him. I fear, however, that his terms will remain the same. He is not a man who cares overmuch for any other than close friends."

Brinsley nodded. "The terms are acceptable, Ashley. You shall become a full partner in Brinsley Enterprises. Please understand that, if such a thing must be, I prefer you as a partner above all others. My only reluctance stems from the fact that the business has never had an owner other than a Brinsley."

A tight smile on his lips, the agent nodded in understanding. "Thank you, sir. I shall leave immediately to call upon my friend. It will, I believe, save much time if I meet with you at your home when I find whether I am able to recall your earlier refusal."

"My home? I fail to understand the necessity of that. The matter has to do with the business. I would prefer to discuss it here, rather than con-

217

cern my wife and daughter with such matters. The abduction of the duchess has them unstrung at the moment. I would not add to their worry."

"I quite understand, sir. However I must insist. I would speak of matters not related to the business and would have both ladies present at the speaking."

Frowning, Brinsley hesitated a moment before saying, "Very well, Ashley. I shall meet you at the house. Will you be long in discovering whether your friend will again make the offer?"

The tight smile returned to Currante's lips. "I shall endeavor to speed up the matter as much as possible. Now, if there is nothing else, I should take myself to him in all haste."

"Of course, by all means hurry, man."

"May he be in a generous mood, Sir Reginald," Currante answered as he left the business.

"May he indeed," Brinsley echoed.

"You are certain you will be able to gain the upper floor of the place?" the earl asked as the carriage neared The Devil's Pit.

Boyden's eyes hardened. "The prostitutes have their rooms there, sir. I shall assume the role of the man who only yesterday was in search of such pleasures of the flesh. Failing that, I will force my way through the place. With Carrie's very life at stake I will brook no interference from anyone who occupies the Pit."

The earl nodded thoughtfully. Finally he said, "It would serve you well to enter alone and partake of several grogs before acting. Should the three of us enter as a group, our purpose would be realized. Parkins and I will follow minutes later and hope no one becomes suspicious."

"Considering that, sir, I believe it would serve better, since I am known to the bartender, if you and Parkins would enter first, purchase a measure of grog, and take a seat at a table. I shall follow in ten minutes and remain at the bar. I feel there will be less chance of any supposing you are with me if we use such an approach."

"You are correct," the earl said. "You have the requirements of a first-class investigator. Parkins and I shall become two old friends seeking nothing but pleasure and reflection on our past escapades. It is settled."

Boyden called to the driver and, when the carriage had come to a stop, nodded to his companions. "It is but a short walk from this point, sirs. I shall follow on foot, lest someone notice the three of us stepping from the same carriage."

The earl extended his hand, saying, "Good fortune to you, Brett. Let us this day see the safe return of our dear friend Carrie." With that he spoke to the driver and the carriage moved away, leaving Boyden behind.

* * *

The earl and the investigator were seated at a corner table of the inn when Boyden entered. Neither of the men glanced in his direction but kept their heads close together talking. As Boyden ordered ale from the same bartender he had spoken to previously, raucous laughter came from the corner. He turned to glance in the direction of the earl and the investigator.

"There would appear to be good spirits about today," he said, turning his attention back to the bartender. "For my own, I prefer the beauty I spoke of yesterday, sir. Is she about?"

The bartender, too, glanced at the two men, then back to Boyden as he placed the ale on the counter. "Those two attempt to recall the past, unless I mistake it," he said in answer to Boyden's statement.

"Which many would if possible," Boyden returned. "What of the lass I intended to use yesterday, sir? Is she available?"

The unshaven face twisted into a frown. "She tired of the long thirty minutes it took you, sir. She and the others have taken the day to themselves."

"She is in one of the rooms above?"

The bartender shook his head. "There is no one present save myself and the customers you see here, sir. As I have said, all others have taken the day for themselves."

Forcing an expression of disappointment on his

face, Boyden drank of the ale and asked, "And are they of such wealth they can forfeit a day's income at their choosing?"

"It was not of their choosing" was the answer. "No more so than the early closing hour ordered is mine."

"Ah, the authorities have seen to the last of it, have they?"

"Hardly that," the man growled. "No, it is the wish of the owner that this day be shortened by the evening hours. God alone knows why."

Finishing his ale, Boyden ordered another and, when the bartender turned to get it, said, "I believe I shall venture to the upper floor in case the lovely one has returned without your knowledge." So saying, he moved quickly to the stairs and up.

"What?" came the startled demand from behind him. Then, "Hold. You cannot go up there this day. Stop, I say."

Ignoring the call, Boyden moved upward at a steady pace. He was nearing the top of the stair when he heard the bartender call the names of three men, saying, "Take the bloke and break his stupid neck. Hurry!"

The sounds of movement brought him around only two steps from the upper floor. His body was tensed and ready for battle as he faced the thugs coming toward him.

"I believe that will do, gentlemen," came the calm voice of the earl, bringing the three to a stop.

He and Parkins stepped to the foot of the stair with guns drawn and faces angry. "There'll be no attacking a gentleman for his money this day."

"This is of no concern of yours," the bartender growled at them, his hand going beneath the bar. "Take yourselves back to your exploration of the past, lest you find trouble you do not have the belly for." His hand reappeared holding a huge horse pistol. Without further word he brought the flint to full cock and aimed it at the earl.

The earl smiled at him. "You are correct, sir." He allowed the barrel of his drawn pistol to droop an inch, then quickly swung it back up and fired.

The bartender took the ball in the shoulder and screamed. The horse pistol dropped to the surface of the bar and discharged harmlessly into the far wall of the inn. Then the earl took Parkins's pistol from him and held it steady on the thugs who stood staring at the wounded bartender.

"Make no mistake, buckos," he warned them. "I am not one to fool with the likes of you. Hold your places and bat not one eye if you wish to continue using the bodies you find yourselves in." Then, without taking his glance from them, he called, "Have your look, Brett. There are none here who will question your right to do so."

Chuckling, Brett gained the upper floor and made his way along the hall, opening door after door. When he arrived at the only door with a bar on it, he smiled momentarily, braced himself, and kicked the portal inward.

Silent darkness met him from within the room. Cautiously he stepped across the threshold, calling, "Carrie, are you here?" Then a glancing blow struck him alongside the head and pitched him sideways.

"Now, you blighter," came a coarse voice from the darkness to his left, "we'll see what you are about with the firing of guns below."

Shaking his head, Boyden rose to his hands and knees just as the attacker stepped between him and the dim light coming from the hallway. He threw himself up and forward, his fists doubled into clubs, his mind consumed with felling his enemy.

His outstretched fists struck flesh and drew a grunt from the attacker. Then he had the man by the throat and pushed him backward to the open door. Seconds later, with the hall light to aid him, he sent a numbing blow to the man's Adam's apple and stepped back.

The thug dropped to the rough flooring of the hallway, his breath coming in hoarse, rasping gasps. His hands clutched at the aching throat.

"I would not be further bothered with one such as you," Boyden said, swinging a measured kick to the rear of the man's head.

The head dropped to the floor and the eyes remained closed as the assailant rolled into unconsciousness. Ignoring the fallen adversary, Boyden turned to reenter the room.

He again called the duchess's name and heard the unmistakable thump of feet against wood flooring. Closing his eyes tightly to shut out all light, he stood several seconds, then opened them. To his right he could discern a bulk darker than the surrounding darkness. A sigh of relief left his lungs then, and he made his way forward to remove the bonds holding the duchess.

"Ah, Brett," she exclaimed as the gag dropped from her lips, "the salvation I prayed for came in a manner I had not expected. How did you discover my whereabouts?"

"Chance guess, Carrie," he answered, working at the bonds holding her hands. "I have ever been the one to follow my suspicions."

"And thank God for such a thing, Brett," she said in relief. "I have information that will surprise all concerned."

"Take your ease, Carrie," he suggested as he bent to work at the bonds holding her feet. "Currante, who owns this place, is the guilty party. He has ventured too far this day. We shall see to the man's undoing."

"You knew he owned this brothel?"

"I surmised it after visiting it yesterday. Something the bartender mentioned brought me to the belief that Currante was more than a lackey for your grandson."

"Much more," she agreed. "An abductor among other things. We must make haste. Even now he is on his way to loan the money to Reginald in return for a partnership in Brinsley Enterprises—and in addition Melissa's hand in marriage."

The words stilled Boyden's fingers. His gray eyes came up to meet her green ones. "The man shall dine with the devil ere this day is done," he muttered. He again began working at the knots, adding, "Concern yourself not, Carrie. No contract taken in such a manner will hold with the authorities. The man will find himself devoid of all profit from this scheme before many more hours."

"True," she answered as the bonds fell to the floor. "However I would make the truth known to Reginald at the earliest possible moment. The stolen funds have all this time been hidden at the site of Currante's rooms. Currante told me this himself. Besides stealing the sixty-two thousand pounds, he used Brinsley money to purchase this brothel. The man is despicable."

"Come, Carrie," Brett said, "let us go to the lower floor where Charlie and his investigator await our coming. Your friend has this day saved both our beings, unless I misguess."

"Ah, Charlie," she said softly. "I might have known he would have a part in this." She allowed Brett to take her arm then and lead her from the room.

CHAPTER TWENTY-TWO

Brinsley entered his home to face his wife and daughter. The expression on the women's faces spoke of their worry for the duchess.

"Father," Melissa asked as soon as he had entered, "what of Grandmother?"

"Yes, Reginald," his wife echoed, "tell us."

"There is nothing as yet to report," he told them. "Even now Ashley is speaking with his friend in an attempt to again make the money available to me. Other than that all events stand as they were when I left."

"Have you spoken with Brett, Father?" Melissa asked.

"Boyden? Why, no, I haven't seen the man since his departure earlier. Why? Is there something he has found to assist us?"

Melissa shook her head sadly. "No, Father, It is only that I believed we would hear from him before this. I was certain he would discover something to lead him to Grandmother."

Crossing to place his hand on the girl's arm, Brinsley said, "Though I know nothing of what you and he have shared, Melissa, I would have you know that he is but a man. His offer to assist if he were able is taken kindly by me. But bear in mind that he is a Colonist. You would do well to consider others for the giving of your heart."

She reddened in anger at the advice. "Such as Ashley Currante?" she demanded. "There was no mention of partnership in Brett's offer of assistance, Father. I fail to see why you consider him beneath Ashley."

"True, child," he answered. "And though his offer was a generous one—without demands—it was at the same time empty of money. Any man can say with ease that his money would be mine, if he were sure there was no way the offer could be accepted."

"That is unfair, Reginald," Lady Brinsley said. "There is no doubt in my mind that Mr. Boyden and his offer were genuine. Judging from Ashley's methods, as they have been revealed by Melissa, I find myself wondering anew at his value, whether as a husband or as a partner."

"Bah!" Brinsley exclaimed. "The partnership was not his idea. As for his actions toward Melissa, I'm certain they amounted to no more than that of any other young man taken by a lass. Young love requires certain methods, Mother."

"He is a beast," Melissa said. "How can you talk so?"

Turning to her, he smiled sympathetically. "Ah,

Melissa, you have been so protected from life. Men, when taken by one such as you, lose control of themselves. It is a point you should be proud of. Not many are capable of making men lose their minds in such a manner."

"Nor do many care to be, unless I misguess," she retorted. "I shall be in my room if news of Grandmother or of Brett should be forthcoming." She turned to leave and met the butler coming into the room to announce that Mr. Ashley Currante had arrived.

"Stay yourself, Melissa," Sir Brinsley ordered. Then to the butler he added, "Show the man in."

"I see no reason to be present, Father," Melissa said, dreading another meeting with the agent.

"Ashley asked that both you and your mother be present, Melissa," her father informed her. "He has his reasons, I am certain." His attention went to the parlor door as Ashley Currante stepped into the room with a smile on his face. "Ah, Ashley, what news, man?"

"Lord Brinsley, Lady Brinsley, Melissa," Currante greeted with a slight bow. "I have spoken to my friend. The loan will be made available under the aforementioned terms—plus one other."

"Thank God," Brinsley sighed.

"What one other?" Melissa demanded, her eyes narrowed in suspicion.

"Eh, what?" Brinsley asked, coming out of his

reverie. "Yes, man, what other term is there to be?"

Currante's lips bent into a dry smile. His glance settled on Melissa. "The term is my own, Sir Reginald, with the agreement of my friend. As well as becoming a full partner in Brinsley Enterprises, I will require the hand of Melissa in marriage as a portion of the loan contract."

"What?" Lady Brinsley gasped.

"You jest, man," Brinsley said. "You mean to force—"

"I make myself plain, sir," Currante interrupted. "The money is available, but only on the terms I have stated. The choice is yours."

"You are loathsome," Melissa growled. "You think it possible to force me into marriage with you? Never. I would rather die."

A bitter chuckle escaped his lips. "But it is not you who shall die as I understand it, Melissa. Your decision, I believe, also decides the fate of the duchess, does it not?"

Melissa paled at the words. Her glance went to her father, who stood stock still with an open mouth, staring at Currante.

"I cannot believe my ears, Ashley," Lady Brinsley said, coming forward to face him. "You can't be serious in this demand."

The tight smile became a sneer as he met her glance. "Your hearing has not fled you, madam. Though it is obvious there are none here who think of me in a respectful mood, the terms are as I have stated. The choice rests with you."

Brinsley turned to face his daughter, an expression of defeat in his eyes. "Ah, Melissa, I—"

"No, Father," she sobbed. "I cannot. I—"

"The duchess is of no consequence to me, Melissa," Currante said. "You know I make no jest with such a demand on you. As to the business, half a loaf is better than none. Is it not, Sir Reginald?"

"You are insufferable," Brinsley got out. "Grandmother was correct in her judgment of you, sir. You ask too much."

"Very well," Currante said, again bowing. "I am certain the duchess would, if she were able, agree with what you say." He turned to leave. "Good afternoon, sir. I must advise my friend as to the nature of the situation."

"Wait . . ." Melissa got out, her hand at her throat.

The agent turned, his black eyes glinting in satisfaction. "Yes, Melissa?"

"I"—she looked plaintively to her mother and father—"I will become your wife, Mr. Currante."

"Mr. Currante?" he asked in a sarcastic tone.

Lowering her head, she muttered, "Ashley. I agree to become your wife, Ashley."

"Ah, excellent," he answered, crossing to her. "Then with your kiss of good fortune on my lips I shall return to my friend and secure the needed money. Kiss me, Melissa."

Her head came up as his hands settled on her shoulders. Her eyes met his through her tears and she stepped forward to place her lips against his. When the embrace ended, he stepped back, a chuckle coming to his lips, his hands still resting on her shoulders.

She met his glance. "Though I shall marry you, Ashley," she said, "know that I loathe you and always shall. Were it not for Grandmother, I would never in all my life allow you to touch me."

"And that, too, shall change, darling," he said. "A pity there are circumstances in life that offer no likable alternative."

"But likable or not, there is *always* an alternative," Brett Boyden said from the parlor doorway.

Currante spun to face the younger man. For an instant anger swept all other expressions from his face. Then suddenly he laughed. "Ah, the Colonist. Tell me, Boyden, have you no well wishes for Melissa and me? She has this moment consented to be my wife."

"Because of fear for her grandmother's life?" Boyden demanded without moving.

Currante nodded. "Whatever the reason the marriage shall be to my liking."

"I had no choice, Brett," Melissa got out. "I—"

"There is always a choice, Missy," he answered, the beginning of a smile on his face.

231

Brinsley stepped forward to face Boyden. "Tell me, man, do your words mean you have found a method of undoing all that has gone before without the sacrifices we now face?"

"I do, sir," Boyden answered. "The simplest solution to your situation is to discover the true thief and abductor and expose him to the authorities. There is little doubt the money would then be located and all else cleared up."

"Impossible," Brinsley said. "The thief killed himself. As for the abductors, they will kill the duchess if they do not receive their ransom by tomorrow evening."

"I fear I must disagree with you, Sir Reginald," Boyden chuckled. Then over his shoulder he said, "Duchess, what are your feelings on the matter?"

The duchess stepped into the room and sent a scathing glance at Currante before saying, "I feel as you do, Brett. There would be no problem if the truth concerning Mr. Currante were made public."

"Grandmother!" Melissa exclaimed in disbelief. Then, her face breaking into a smile of happiness, she started toward the old woman.

She was brought up short by Currante's strong hand settling harshly on her arm. Roughly he pulled her into the circle of his arm. At the same moment his right hand came from his pocket holding the small pistol he had pointed at the duchess earlier.

The barrel of the weapon settled against Melissa's temple, and he said to all present, "One move wrongly done and she dies on the spot." His eyes bored into Boyden's. "You, Colonist, seem to have worked a minor miracle. Well, it will avail you nothing. Your precious Melissa will leave with me. If you or anyone else wish to see her alive again, you will offer no resistance to my leave taking."

Boyden, his gray eyes glittering deadly, nodded. "You are—while holding the gun—in charge, Currante. But listen and heed my words: Should anything in the way of injury at your hand befall Melissa, I'll follow you to the ends of the earth to have your life."

Currante laughed at the threat. "You frighten me, Colonist. Now, Brinsley, I would have a carriage at the front stoop immediately."

His face drawn in fear and shock, Brinsley said, "The carriage shall be there, Ashley. My God, man, you wouldn't harm her."

The laugh came again to the agent. "As quickly as I snuffed out the life of Wright, you idiot. Do you take me for a soft heart? Her time draws nearer with every moment you delay me. The carriage, now!"

"Do it," Boyden ordered, his glance steady on Currante.

Brinsley offered no further resistance. Turning, he hurried from the parlor, calling to the butler to have a carriage brought around. Moments later he returned to the parlor and told Currante, "It is being done. Take the carriage and whatever else you like, man. I'll not begrudge anything, only do not harm Melissa."

The wicked gleam in the black eyes deepened. "You judge me for a fool, Brinsley? Hah! When the carriage is prepared, all here will accompany me to the front stoop. Melissa and I shall then take the carriage and be gone. Her very existence depends upon all of you and the restraint you can muster. Do I make myself clear?"

"If the old duke were alive at this moment, he would have your head, sir," the duchess growled, her brows knitted into an angry line.

"But he is not," Currante retorted. "And it is Melissa's life at stake this moment, not mine."

"You are making one fatal mistake, Currante," Boyden said, his voice soft. "I judged you more intelligent than that."

"The authorities?" Currante demanded with a laugh. "To accomplish their duties the authorities must be informed of the crime. Melissa's life depends on none of you so informing them."

"I spoke not of the authorities, but of myself," Boyden corrected him. "You err in that respect."

"How so?" came the question. "You mean to indicate that you doubt my intent to kill this precious one of yours should anyone interfere?"

Boyden shook his head in a negative answer. "I

meant you should kill me now, else I shall see to your death before this event ends."

The harsh laugh came again, and Currante said, "You do expect everyone to be as foolish as yourself, Colonist. You would have me spend the one ball at my disposal in hopes that I would miss you and leave myself open to capture. I admire your thinking, but I am not the fool you suppose."

The butler entered the parlor at that moment and stopped in his tracks, his eyes wide, his mouth open as he stared at the scene unfolding there.

Brinsley turned to him and snapped, "Well, man, is the carriage ready?"

The butler nodded in answer. His mouth closed, opened again; then without uttering a word, he turned as if to leave.

"Stay yourself, lackey," Currante called. "You, too, shall accompany us to the stoop. Now, all of you, ahead of me and remember: Any false motion will bring instant death to this dear one of yours."

"Do as he says," Boyden ordered, turning to lead the way from the parlor.

"Now," Currante ordered as they reached the stoop, "all of you step aside out of reach of me as I pass." When they moved to obey, he stepped through the opening, pushing Melissa ahead of him, to fix the carriage driver with his eyes. "You, driver, do you know this woman I hold pistol to?"

"Aye, sir," the driver said, a stricken expression

on his features. "Since she was a tot, I've known her. What are you about, sir?"

"Hush," came the command. "You will drive to the gate and stop for my order as to our destination. Any attempt by you to call attention to anyone along our route will result in a ball entering the head of this female. Do you understand?"

The driver sent a glance at Brinsley and nodded. "Aye, sir. Just you take care with that pistol."

"Just you remember where the pistol is placed," Currante said. Then to Melissa he added, "You may open the carriage door, my dear."

Stark fear shown in the girl's eyes as she reached to do as she was told. As the carriage door came open she asked, "What—what will you do with me?"

Currante chuckled and pushed her into the carriage, holding the pistol steady on her as he did so. "You and the others may well spend your time wondering as to the answer to that," he snarled, following her into the carriage. Then, with the gun covering her, he pushed her to the seat and ordered, "Close the door, my dear, and let us be off."

Bending to clutch the door, Melissa suddenly threw herself forward, attempting to leave the carriage. The hand holding the pistol moved swiftly and the metal of the weapon struck her on the head, driving her back into the seat.

Currante turned to look down into the angry eyes of Boyden, who had moved violently forward at the attack. "Close the door, you fool, before I do more than simply convince her of her foolishness." The gun was level on the girl's sobbing figure.

"Your wish is my command," Boyden said bitterly, closing the carriage door.

"Now step back," Currante commanded. When Boyden had done as ordered, Currante called to the driver, "Away, now."

The carriage moved away from the safety of Brinsley House that had been Melissa's home for all the years of her life.

As the carriage rolled along the drive, away from the assemblage on the stoop, Boyden turned to Brinsley, asking, "Where, in your estimation, would he most likely head for, sir?"

Reluctantly pulling his eyes from the receding carriage, Brinsley turned to face him. "What? I have no idea. Why? There is nothing—nothing we can do but pray that he does not harm my daughter."

An expression of rising disgust settled on the younger man's features. "You fool yourself if you believe he will ever allow her to leave him alive, sir. The man is desperate at this moment and will remain so until captured. Now, think. Where would he head for first?"

"Answer him, Reginald," the duchess ordered. "There is no pity in Currante. He informed me while I was held captive that my life would be forfeited no matter what took place. Every minute you hesitate brings Missy closer to meeting her maker."

"I—I don't know," Brinsley answered, tears glowing in his eyes. "The man is mad. We must do as he has ordered."

Boyden's eyes narrowed in thought. Suddenly he reached to clutch Brinsley's shoulders asking, "Did he make a show of the money he was to loan you, sir?"

"What? No, he had only made known his demands when you and—"

"Then, there is a possibility he did not bring the money with him," Boyden interrupted, turning to face the duchess. "Carrie, you said he used his rooms as a hiding place for the stolen funds, did you not?"

She nodded. "So he informed me while I was held captive, Brett. Do you suppose he will go there now?"

"If, indeed, the money is there, he will make that his first stop. He would not attempt to leave England or the city without it, especially since he is aware that you know of its whereabouts." Turning back to Brinsley, he snapped, "I will require a pistol and a horse, sir. Now."

Lady Brinsley, until that moment held silent by

near panic at her daughter's abduction, sobbed, "You cannot, sir. He will certainly kill her if anyone should offer him resistance."

"And he will do the same if no one resists," Boyden retorted. "Brinsley, the pistol and the horse. Else I shall be forced to send a message to the authorities and pray that they are not as bumblesome as is their usual wont."

"You would not," Brinsley got out. "You—"

"I, sir, love your daughter more than anything in this world. I refuse to allow her death because of the orders of some madman."

"Reginald!" the duchess snapped. "Find a pistol for him and see to his need for a horse. Do it, you fool, else you shall stand no chance of seeing Missy alive again."

His features sagging in defeat, Brinsley ordered the butler to prepare a mount, then turned to enter the house. Behind him filed his wife, the duchess, and Boyden. "I have but the one weapon," he said to no one in particular. "It is in the library." He stepped away from them as if in a trance and entered the mentioned room. Several minutes later he returned to hand Boyden a slim pistol of French dueling design. "The charge is old, I fear. I have never had reason to fire it."

"It will serve, I pray," Boyden answered, accepting the pistol and turning back to the doorway.

"Brett," the duchess called. When he had halted

and turned to face her, she said, "Bring her back to us, Brett. We love her as you do."

"Such is my intent, Carrie. I shall do so or die in the attempt." Then he was gone.

Moments later the beat of a horse's hooves came to the three people who stood in silent fear and wonder.

"Her chance is as good at this moment as it will ever be," the duchess said matter-of-factly. "If anyone can accomplish her rescue, it is Brett Boyden."

"I pray that you are correct, Grandmama," Brinsley muttered, reaching to place an arm around his wife's shoulders. "Now we can but wait for news of whatever is to happen."

The duchess suddenly straightened and faced him directly. "While you wait, Reginald, you would do well to reassess your thoughts concerning Brett. When he returns with Melissa, you will be faced with the decision of losing her forever or agreeing to a marriage between her and Brett."

Brinsley met her demanding eyes and nodded. "There is little question in my mind but that I have ill-judged the man, Grandmama. If, indeed, he can save Melissa from Ashley's clutches, I shall abide by her decision." His expression darkened, and he added, "I fear there is little hope for the success of his venture."

"Then you are indeed a fool," she told him. "Brett Boyden stated his intent perfectly when he said he would rescue her or lose his own life in the attempt. Cease your underrating of the man. He is as near like the old duke as anyone with whom I have become acquainted. Have faith."

"The events of this day have unstrung me, I fear," he answered, his glance going to his wife. "Edith, too, has given up hope of ever seeing Melissa again."

"Take her and yourself and your negative thoughts away from me," the duchess said. "I will wait the arrival of Missy and Brett alone." She turned to enter the parlor, leaving the Brinsleys to themselves.

CHAPTER TWENTY-THREE

Upon leaving Brinsley property, Boyden set heels to the horse and raced toward Currante's domicile. The pistol in his waistband rubbed harshly against his flesh, but he was unaware of it as his thoughts centered on what must occur should he be fortunate enough to have guessed correctly in his evaluation of Ashley Currante.

Heads turned as he raced along the city street, unmindful of anyone foolish enough to step into his path. He was oblivious to the curses flung at him by one who leapt for his life, barely dodging the racing hooves of the horse. Then, after what seemed an eternity, he swung the horse around a corner and saw the Brinsley carriage in position at the front of Currante's building.

Dismounting, he allowed the horse loose rein and stepped quickly to the side of the carriage to speak to the driver who sat as if paralyzed.

"Quickly, man," Boyden demanded, "what of Currante and Melissa?"

The driver's head turned, and he looked down at Boyden with vacant eyes. "He has her, sir," he mumbled. "Took the lass into that door there and ordered me to wait. He intends to kill her should any block his way."

Boyden nodded in understanding. "We shall do our level best to prevent such a happening, shan't we? Apply whip to your horses and report to the nearest authorities. Bring them here immediately. I shall visit Mr. Currante's rooms and see to our destinies." With that, he turned away and entered the building. He was only vaguely aware of the sound of the carriage leaving as he made his way up the steps to the door of the agent's flat.

Once he had gained the door, he hesitated long enough to lay an ear to the panel and assure himself that human movement was discernible from within. Then he drew the pistol from his belt, sprung the flint back into firing position, and with one well-placed kick drove the door inward. He was moving even as the panel flung open.

Ashley Currante stood but three feet inside the door. In his left hand he held a package, in his right, the pistol. The pistol was pointed directly at Melissa, who stood next to him.

"Hold, Currante," Boyden ordered, bringing the dueling pistol to bear on the man.

For a moment, panic shone from the black eyes. Then bitterness filled the face, and Currante said, "You are a fool, Boyden. Nothing has changed but that you have touched my anger. I shall take that anger out on your beloved Melissa for your impudence. Now drop that weapon and move out of our way, else you will have her blood on your hands."

Boyden allowed the beginning of a bitter smile to pull at the corner of his lips. "You err again, Currante," he said in an even voice. "The flintlock must be drawn back in order that the gun might fire."

"Your trick will not work with me," Currante snarled. Then, as if against all the will he had, his eyes flicked to the pistol he held to Melissa.

In the instant the eyes moved, Boyden released the flint of the French dueling pistol and the room filled with the weapon's echoing roar. Currante stood as if frozen for three heartbeats. Then, his eyes rolling backward into his head, he collapsed to the floor.

Melissa stood in awe, her glance on the fallen abductor. Her features paled, and with a sigh she sank to the floor in a faint.

Boyden moved forward, not to Melissa but to the still form of Currante. Reversing the gun in his hand, he raised it as a club and bent to turn the body on its back. He relaxed as he saw the blood seep from a hole in the agent's temple. An instant later he was beside Melissa, cradling her in his arms and calling her name softly. He was like that when the doorway was filled by men wearing the insignia of the Crown's authority.

"Welcome, gentlemen," he said, mustering a

smile. "Your search for a murderer and an abductor has ended." He indicated Currante with a sweep of his hand and added, "He is beyond the point of misjudging anyone again."

For a moment the leader of the officers stood silently, sending his glance around the room. Then he moved forward to ask, "And is the lady injured, sir?"

Boyden shook his head. "She has fainted, I fear. Concern yourself not about her. She is in my care. See to the body of that one there. Unless I misguess, the package beside him contains the money stolen from Sir Reginald Brinsley. You would do well to see that it is returned to him at the soonest." He stood then, lifting Melissa's unconscious form in his arms. "Has the Brinsley carriage returned?"

"It has, sir. The driver insisted on returning, though we advised otherwise" was the answer as the men of the Crown moved to study Currante's body.

"Then, if I have your approval, I shall return Melissa to her parents," Boyden said, already moving toward the doorway with the girl in his arms.

Stepping aside, the officer raised a hand in salute, saying, "Of course, sir. And if I may, sir, you've done a fine day's work."

Boyden only nodded in answer as he stepped from the room and made his way toward the stairs. A moment later he stepped into the sunshine of the day and sent his glance at the driver of the carriage. "It is done," he said, moving toward the carriage.

As if afraid of an answer the driver asked, "And the child, sir. Is she dead?"

Boyden laughed in relief. "No, my good man, she has only fainted. Now take the reins and deliver us to her parents in the shortest possible time." He turned, sending a glance back down the street. "What of the steed that brought me here?"

The smile that broke the face of the driver made his relief obvious. "Taken care of, sir. No one would concern himself with worry over the beast at any rate."

Placing Melissa in the carriage, Boyden nodded in understanding. "You are correct. Their daughter and her safety fill their minds at this moment. Quickly, man, to Brinsley House." He jumped into the carriage and knelt to lay a loving palm against the girl's cheek.

Her eyes fluttered open under his touch, and she asked, "Oh, Brett, where are we?"

"In a carriage bound for Brinsley House, my love," he answered, bending to place his lips on hers. When the embrace ended, he pulled back and she came to a sitting position in the seat, asking, "What happened, Brett? What of Ashley Currante?"

"He is dead, Missy. The money stolen from your

246

father is now in the hands of the authorities and will shortly find its way back to Brinsley coffers. Do not concern yourself with such things. You have been through a great deal."

"He was evil, Brett. I have never met such an evil man as he."

He nodded in agreement, then looked away.

"Something is the matter," she said. "What is it, Brett?"

"I have said I wish you for a wife, Melissa," he answered. "I intend speaking of it to your father when we arrive at Brinsley House. But you must know something. Anyone who becomes my wife will of necessity return to the United States with me. I have not asked your feelings on the matter."

Her laugh was like the tinkling of silver bells. Reaching to lay a hand on his arm, she said, "Ah, Brett, do you not know that I would follow you into the pits of Hades if such were required to be near you. I will love your country as you do. We shall be happy beyond our wildest dreams."

His gray eyes met hers and came alive at the words. He reached for her and drew her to him in a deep embrace. They were like that when the carriage drew to a stop at the front of Brinsley House.

No sooner had the wheels of the carriage stopped than the door of the house flew open and the Brinsleys and the duchess rushed out. Relief and happiness filled their three faces as they swept to the carriage, calling Melissa's name.

Boyden released the girl, saying, "And now, dear one, it is time for you to show your family that you are in one piece."

She turned from him and stepped from the carriage into the waiting arms of Lady Brinsley. A moment later tears were flowing from the eyes of both women. Behind them Brinsley and the duchess raised grateful eyes to Boyden.

"My thanks, sir," Brinsley managed in choked greeting. "You have this day delivered our most precious possession to us. I will never be able to thank you enough."

The duchess smiled and stepped forward to offer Brett her hand. "Well done, Brett. I had no doubt that if it would be accomplished you would do it. What of Currante?"

"Dead," Boyden told her. "As any of his ilk should be in such an instance."

"And the stolen money?" Brinsley asked.

Boyden nodded. "Safe in the care of the authorities, sir. It should be returned to you in a short time."

"Well," Brinsley said, turning to take his daughter's arm, "come into the house. We can better discuss the matter in comfort over tea."

CHAPTER TWENTY-FOUR

When they had all seated themselves in the parlor and tea had been served, Boyden related the events of Melissa's rescue. When he had finished, he looked at the cup in his hand, and then tipped it upside down to drain it.

"A man the old duke would have been proud of," the duchess exclaimed. "Ah, Brett, such fortune we have that you were here at the moment this thing happened. Had it not been for you, who can say what might have occurred."

"It was nothing, Carrie," he said. "It was my pleasure to be of service to you."

"But," Lady Brinsley said, "there must be a method whereby we can show our appreciation to you, sir. In my lifetime no one has served us in such a manner. We are truly grateful."

He met her sincere glance, and then swung his eyes to Brinsley. "There is one way," he said. "I would have your blessings on my marriage to your daughter."

Silence held the Brinsleys for a moment, then Brinsley looked to the duchess, saw the smile on her face, and said, "As you informed us, Grandmama." He brought his attention back to Boyden, a smile on his lips. "Though I have all this time considered you a Colonist, sir, you are everything the duchess and Melissa have said of you. I take pleasure in welcoming you to the Brinsley family. You have the blessings you ask."

A small squeal of happiness escaped Melissa's lips. She jumped from her seat and rushed to her father to throw her arms about him. "Oh, Father," she sighed, "I am the happiest and luckiest woman in the entire world. Thank you."

Lady Brinsley asked, "And, Mr. Boyden, will you be taking Melissa to America once you are married?"

He nodded. "I will, madam. My business and my life are there. Do not concern yourself, though. Melissa shall return to visit her England as often as she wishes. I would hope that all of you will someday soon see fit to making a visit to my country as well."

"An excellent idea," the duchess said. "For one of my age it will be a delightful trip, I am certain. Perhaps I can persuade Charlie to accompany me on such a journey."

"Oh, Grandmother, you are wonderful," Melissa said, leaving her father to go to the old woman's side.

"Of course," the duchess said. "Everyone present is wonderful on this occasion. Well, what now? Are we to have a grand wedding for these two, Reginald?"

"Of course, Grandmama," Brinsley said, getting to his feet. "The grandest affair London has been privy to in many years."

"A formal ball," Lady Brinsley said. "Yes, a grand ball for our daughter's wedding." She stood, her manner hurried. "I must begin preparations this moment."

Boyden, a smile on his face at the happiness displayed in the room, said, "I fear I must take my leave now. The authorities have requested that I make a full report on Currante's death. Might I borrow your carriage, Sir Reginald?"

"Of course, man. Need you ask?" Brinsley told him, draping an arm over the younger man's shoulder. "Whatever I have is yours for the asking. Come, I will attend the authorities with you."

Boyden nodded in agreement. "There is a site known as The Devil's Pit I believe you should see, sir," he said. "It seems the place will, when all is settled, become your property. You should apply your thoughts to its future."

"The Devil's Pit?" Brinsley asked. "How am I to become owner of this place, and what is it?"

The duchess laughed aloud at the question. "Ah, Reginald, I sense you will find yourself taken aback when you discover what Brinsley money has been spent on by Currante. Tell him, Brett. Then the two of you take yourselves from us. Edith will need assistance in planning the ball."

Boyden smiled and bowed to her. Then,

251

straightening, he said, "Well, Sir Reginald, it would appear you are about to become the owner of a rather sordid brothel. Come, allow me to show you."

"Brothel!" Brinsley asked, following the younger man from the room. "Brothel?"

Behind the two men the duchess muttered, "Such a man that one is. Such a man."

"My man, Grandmother. All mine," Melissa answered happily. "Forever and ever."

Love—the way you want it!

Candlelight Romances

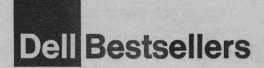